STEVEN L. CASE

FATHER DARK

A NOVEL

the apocryphile press
BERKELEY, CA
www.apocryphile.org

apocryphile press
BERKELEY, CA

Apocryphile Press
1700 Shattuck Ave #81
Berkeley, CA 94709
www.apocryphile.org

Printed in the United States of America
ISBN 978-1-937002-84-8

DEDICATION

This book is dedicated to the memory of my mother Mary Case. She would have hated it. But she would have shown it off at every committee meeting, group gathering, and to random strangers. "Look what my son wrote." She would have kept it in that box with all the Crayola drawings, spelling tests, and articles I've written over the years. She gave me a passion for words and a love for good stories. She never stopped bragging about her sons and if Amazon delivers to heaven I'm sure Jesus is already tired of hearing about it by now.

ACKNOWLEDGEMENTS

Becky Case: For love and patience beyond reason

Aprille Case, Eric Case:
for listening to stories about Wally and Cheeto

John Metcalf: For being a brony

John Mabry: For taking the risk

Padi Hallum Joseph: For the name

Kirk Moore: Who said, "I know a guy...."

Mark Oestreicher:
For Dedication and Opportunities

Sid Case: For letting Brian and me
set up Hot-Wheels in the sanctuary

Rev. Majorie Gerbracht-Stagnero:
Who should be a Saint for constant kind words

Christopher Moore: for inspiration,
illumination and the phrase "dirt-side"

Russell Thorndike: for inspiration

Diane Szuch and Larry Ciferno: who said,
"You should think about being a writer."

The Walt Disney Company:
for creating Scarecrow of Romney Marsh

Trader Joes: For no reason
but I thought they might throw me some
coffee and chocolate for the mention. I consumed
enough during the writing of this book

Bigfinish.com (subscribers get more)

Leroy Hudson—Pierpont Ohio: Maker of Syrup

CHAPTER ONE

I really hate to be the one who has to break this to you, but there are assholes in heaven too.

You ask any guardian who's ever had a dirt-side assignment, and they'll tell you the number one rule of guardian angel office politics is...don't piss off Gabriel. Gabriel has these little ways of reminding you who exactly is in charge. He refers to them as his little pranks. Honestly, it would be a lot easier to accept his "little pranks" if he showed any other sign of having a sense of humor. *Any* sign.

I'm not saying that I didn't deserve it. I have always been a pain in the ass to authority, even when I was alive. But I had one brief shining moment of integrity. One ultimate right-place/ right-time moment where I did the absolute right thing to the absolute right person and I got a hall pass for all eternity. My reward for this this singular act of perfect kindness? Not only did I *not* have to burn in the everlasting fires of hell, but also I get to run errands for the Creator of the Universe.

This is where the manager/employee conflict comes in. I was running errands for *him*. I was *his* servant. A "manager trainee"—who, just because of the nature of the workplace, will never advance any higher and has no possible way to leave the position—doles out assignments. In short, God's favorite angel made up for the fact that he has no sphincter by becoming one.

Gabriel says, "Go," and we go. Usually he gets to recruit who he wants after a long application process, but I was sort of thrust upon him and he had to make do. It was hard at first, so hard that I thought maybe that whole eternal damnation thing wouldn't be so bad. Then Gabriel finally recognized my "special gifts." He started giving me assignments that better matched my "unique job qualifications," and we've actually been able to tolerate each other since then. Not all angels wear white, you know?

I was standing at the edge. I mean that in a literal sense. I was at *the* edge. The spot where the everything starts and the nothingness ends. You may see it one day, but I doubt it. People come up to heaven and spend the first few millennia exploring—millennia being an abstract word here. They go here and there and visit various planes of existence as if they were at Disney World on a perpetual vacation. Then they settle down and find something to occupy their time...which is, in fact, relative. During all their travels, they might hear someone mention the edge. It's the edge of heaven, some say, but that's not really it. The edge isn't like a cliff in a Road Runner cartoon. It's not even an edge that drops off into darkness. It's more like...well, an absence. It's like all of existence just got broken off in this one spot. Nobody comes here. It's not on the big picture map. Even those who considered themselves pretty bad-ass down below don't come here more than once.

Honestly, it's the only place I seem to find peace. I don't like the city. Too much light. People seem to have arrived here and left all of their baggage behind them. There is no hate, no jealousy, no anger, or any other of those things that escaped Pandora's Box. (True story, by the way. Pandora? Nice girl. Little chubby, but a nice girl.)

I go to the City of Light and I feel like I'm a shadow.

I was standing at the edge and I could feel light behind me. I didn't see it illuminate anything in front of me because there was nothing there. The edge did not absorb light—it just sort of made it absent. Okay, I really need to get a better handle on my powers of description. So the light just stopped at my back. I felt him before I saw him.

I said, "Gabriel."

He said, "Micah."

We have that sort of relationship. All warm and fuzzy-like. Gabriel said, "I have an assignment for you."

I could hear him scratching at his clipboard with his little blue Sharpie marker. I know it was blue because I stole all the other colors from his desk. He likes to write on his clipboard when he is doling out assignments.

"You do, or He does?" I asked. Gabriel has a tremendous amount of authority here, but I liked to remind him that he wasn't the ultimate authority.

"He requested you," Gabriel said.

I turned and looked at him. I remember reading the scriptures as a boy. Angels were soldiers with screaming swords and shields of fire and armor that could withstand tanks, had there been any back then. Gabriel always seems to look like an angel from a children's Christmas pageant. He never touches the ground either. His robe always seemed to be hovering just a few inches above it, as if he were afraid he might get dirty if he walked on the same ground with the rest of us. Gabriel, the messenger of God, who had led armies into glorious battle. I wondered what it might take to bring the bad-ass warrior out of him again.

"Where?" I asked.

"Dirt-side."

"I guessed that much," I said. "I mean, where dirt-side?"

"Philadelphia."

"When?"

"Twenty-first century," Gabriel said. "Early on. Perhaps on a Tuesday. Let's say a few hours before dawn."

"I mean," I said, "when does the job start?"

Gabriel smirked at me.

For the record: that trip from earth to heaven...it's all light and love. Going back hurts. It hurts like a son of a bitch.

CHAPTER TWO

A STAR OVER THE I (EYE)
A blog about nothing, written for no one in particular,
by someone who pretty much stopped giving a rat's
ass about things a long time ago.

ENTRY #1
(false start)

ENTRY #2
(false start)

ENTRY #3
(false start)

ENTRY #4
There. Now I can tell the therapist that after several false starts I am indeed blogging. *Court ordered* blogging. Can you believe that? Oh my God. You get totally busted for hacking into your school's computer systems, and after explaining that perhaps it was

because the poor girl spent too much time on the Internet...what do they do? What punishment shall befall this poor girl...a mere victim of society??? You give her a therapist who says, "Padi, I think you should start a blog."

So I start a blog...Hello, world. This is Padi blogging to you. Nobody is going to read this anyway, so I'd like to take this opportunity to say to the good folks in the administration office of Crestview High...Screw you.

There's a reason they call it Crestview Hiiiiiiiiiiiiiiiiiiiigh. It's because the weed situation is rampant...but that's not the problem. Let's solve society's ills by going after the girl who hacked into the system and changed grades. Ooooooo. What a menace she is.

So let's start with the facts. Dr. Conners, my "new BFF" and therapist (Yes, that was sarcasm) said I can write anything I want on my blog as long as it's the truth. Sooo...

Did I change Mike Carney's grade on his senior government term paper? Yes, I did.

There. I said it. Did I lie about it later? Yes, I did. Did I lie about it to my mother? Yes, I did. Did I lie about it to the principal and the board of education and the peer (poetic) justice group? Yes, I did...but as I do not recognize the authority of Crestview's Peer Justice group in this matter, I hardly think their opinion matters.

Mike Carney is a good guy. He struggles but he gets the grades. He works hard and I've never seen him do drugs. He had a part-time job and knew that if he kept working hard he could get a scholarship.

Did Mike Carney write his government term paper, which counts as 40% of the final grade? Yes, he did. I saw it with my own eyes. I held it in my hands as we passed the plastic-covered reports up the row. He did his paper and he turned it in. I saw it. I don't care what Mr. Harper says. I saw it. I held it in my hands.

Mr. Harper says Mike didn't turn it in, and he said so in front of the board, and it wasn't true.

When Mike was told he'd get a zero on the paper he freaked. He was bordering between a B and C anyway. Mr. Harper told him he could print off another copy but he'd still have to take a full grade deduction for being late....*which he wasn't*. Should Mike have found a way to vent his frustrations other than heaving a desk at the wall? Yeah, probably—but under the circumstances...what would you have done?

So Mike gets suspended. He turns in a paper late, which by this point...the most he can hope for is a D. Giving him a good solid C for the year...giving him a 3.3 grade point average...when a 3.5 is needed for a state scholarship.

So....did I hack into the system and change Mike's grade to a B? Yes, did. That's the story. That's the whole story. Mike was my friend and I did him a favor. Everything else you have heard about the situation is a bold-faced lie. (I'm looking at you, Kelsey.)

Mike is now busting his hump while going to a community college, all because Mr. Harper lost his term paper.

Therapist's voice in my head: "Is that true, Padi? Do you know that to be a fact?"

No, I don't. I know Mike turned it in. I don't know

what happened to it after it left the very fingers I'm typing this stupid blog with. There's a whole lot of people who said a whole lot of things about Mike (and me and my MOM, for crying out loud) who said those things without knowing for a fact they were true. Mike's working. I'm finishing the 11th grade in summer school, and in September it starts all over.

There. Dr. Conners said I should start a blog, and I have. Look, Doc, four entries. Is that enough? Can I please go back to writing nasty things about pop-princesses on other people's blogs now?

CHAPTER THREE

When I opened my eyes I realized I was driving. Well, okay, it took a few seconds to realize I was driving and a few more after that to remember how. To go from a place of unconditional love and acceptance, a place where you are warm and happy and embraced by the arms of God, to being instantly human and sitting behind the wheel of a moving vehicle can be jarring. That's what I guess Gabriel was chuckling about. He could have set me down in front of my assignment. He could have simply told me what it was. No. Mr. Glory-Be-To-God puts me in a car. I'm part of the "all things" and then suddenly I'm alone and I'm driving.

At night.

In the dark.

On a highway.

My foot was on what my newly constructed brain told me was the gas. The other pedal was the brake. I stepped on that one. Hard. The car did a three-sixty right there in the middle of the highway. People would be a lot more respectful of other driv-

ers if you could drive this way all the time. Once.
Twice.

I finally came to a stop in the middle of the road,
facing the same direction I had been going in when
I arrived. I inhaled deeply and caught the scent of
the car's heater, road salt, and the yarn in my knit-
ted cap, which I just realized I was wearing. I saw
the snow outside my window and a voice inside my
head said, "winter." Then it added "idiot" just for
fun.

Oh yeah, I remembered driving. I saw city lights
in the distance. "Philadelphia." I said the word out
loud; not from memory, but because it had been
given to me with all the other information so that I
would have it when I needed it. (Another drawback
of working for God's pet: most information was on
a need-to-know basis.)

"Philadelphia." I said it again so I could hear my
"own" voice this time. It sounded middle-aged.
Then again, what is middle-aged these days? You
people live so damn long now. It was a deep voice,
good tone. Maybe I was a singer. Doubtful. Gabriel
liked singers. He had that whole multitude-of-heav-
enly-host thing going on the side. Singers held a
special place in his heart. Hence, I was *not* a singer
this time—but the voice was pretty good.

I looked into the rear view mirror at my eyes.
Those were mine. It was one of the few things that
Gabriel had no control over. No matter who or
where I was...I still got my own eyes. One of the
Big Guy's rules. It was a good one. That way at
least one face was vaguely familiar no matter what
job you had.

The rest of the face was pretty much a younger version of the one I had been assigned last time. It was a good face. I ran my hand over the chin and tested the skin. Little rough. Some stubble. I smiled and the teeth appeared to be all there. I ran my tongue over them and found one missing in the back. I'll say this for Gabriel. He has an attention to detail.

I pulled the car back onto the road and brought it up to speed. I was just sort of cruising along like any other newly arrived motorist outside the City of Brotherly Love. The car was used but clean. Gabriel's usual. There was a crack in the dashboard and one tiny spider web of a crack in the windshield. From the mirror hung one of those air freshener thingies that I took to be one of the details and not a personal criticism. This one was black and had bright gold letters that said, "John 3:16." I guess Gabriel had never heard of Miss January.

In the cup holder was a cup of coffee. *Yes!* I remembered coffee. I took a drink. Old and cold. Gabriel's little attention to details could be annoying. Really, how hard could it be to "poof" a *hot* cup of coffee? Just as easy as for a cold one, I would imagine.

There was a stack of CD's on the passenger seat. I sorted them with one hand. Headlights appeared behind me and I used them to read the CD cases. Most of them were Christian rock. Those I threw on the floor, hoping they might get lost or stepped on. There was one by some guy named Crowder that I hadn't heard of, so I decided to try that one later. There was one Amy Grant. Oh, yes. I remember Amy. I wonder if it's a sin of some kind to have impure thoughts about a beloved Christian singer. There was a disc by a girl named Monica Sunnydale. The picture on the cover depicted Ms. Sunnydale in a shiny pink baseball cap and holding a puppy. The title of the disc was "Son Beam." I used the electric window on the passenger side and allowed Ms. Sunnydale's work to become part of the landscape. At the bottom of the stack was a Rolling Stones disc. I slid it into the mouth of the CD player and *Sympathy for the Devil* began to fill the car. Gabriel may have had a sense of humor after all. Hard to figure out a guy who doesn't let his feet touch the floor.

I rolled the window down and smelled the night. Rolling Stones equals window down. It's a rule. I didn't make it. I turned up the heater a little to compensate. I smelled snow and wet pavement, but there was still just a hint of autumn in the air. Leaves. Perhaps it was November. I'd have to figure that out soon.

I eased the gas pedal down and my glass and metal and I were cruising down the highway as Mick talked about being there when Jesus Christ has his moment of doubt and pain. I sang along at the top of my lungs with, *"Pleased to meet you. Hope you guess my name."* I sang it to the wind and the rain and the car that passed by me on the left leaving my car in the darkness again. It was a good voice.

I heard a horrendous sound and realized it was my stomach. Hungry. I remembered hungry, though it had been a long time. Wind. Cold. Leaves. Stones. Hunger. I liked being human. Pleased to meet you. Hope you guess my name.

Ahead I saw the lights of a truck stop. I stepped on the brake, easier this time, pulled my car off the road onto the truck stop ramp. There wasn't much of crowd. I guessed it was late. I pulled into a parking spot as if I had been driving for years, not minutes. Some things just come back to you. I stepped out of the car and grabbed my own ass to see if I had a wallet. I did. The driver's license said my name was Michael Dark. Pretty close. Pleased to meet you. The picture was pretty good too. I had a lot of hair in the picture. I pulled the stocking cap off and ran my fingers through what I had at the moment. I felt the smooth spot in the back. "Thanks, Gabriel." I put the hat back on and headed for the diner.

For the record, my name is Micah. I'll explain that later. I opened the wallet and found it pretty well stocked with cash and a single credit card. There was a photo of a woman I didn't know. A few business cards including one for someplace called Gabriel's Horns. Real cute.

I opened the door of the truck stop diner and a wave of smells came over me. It was lovely.

There was an immense woman behind the counter. She said, "You lookin' to eat, Father, or are you just lost?"

She was the first human voice I had heard in a very long time. It was a nice voice.

I said, "I'm sorry. What did you say?" I wanted to hear her say it again, both because it was a nice voice and because I swear she called me "Father."

She smiled. It was a nice smile. "I asked if you were lost, Father."

I looked past her to the mirror behind the cash register. My reflection was wearing a clerical collar, which meant that I was too. Cute, Gabriel. Real cute.

She was still waiting for me to answer. I said, "Uhhh...no. Not lost. I'm actually hungry."

She practically beamed at that. "Well come on in and pull up a stool. Do you want to see a menu, or do you know what you're in the mood for?"

I said, "As I recall, blueberry pancakes are quite wonderful."

"Have you been through here before?" she asked. "I have a good memory for faces and I don't remember yours."

She thought I was remembering blueberry pancakes from her place but it was from another time. Another life. I said, "I must be thinking of someplace else."

"Well ours are about the best you're gonna find," she said. "You'll be coming back for ours and you won't ever forget 'em. You want coffee?" Her words ran together like ketchup and mustard on a hamburger bun.

"Yes," I said. "Coffee. Please." Guys in collars are polite, right?

She poured me a cup and sent a note back to the man behind the counter. I could see him through a window cut into the wall. He smiled at me and sort of saluted with his spatula.

I picked up the cup and held it to my nose. Oh, yes, I remembered coffee.

"You gonna drink it or bless it?" she said, and giggled at her own humor.

I sipped the coffee and felt it flow down my throat and warm me into my empty stomach. I felt the heat move out to the ends of my fingers. I looked at her and said, "Ohhhhhhhhhhhh. That's good."

She said, "You been outta the country or somethin'? One of them missions?"

"Something like that," I said.

"People don't usually get that rhapsodic about the coffee."

I smiled at her. She said rhapsodic. A great word. She smiled back and pointed to a "Word of the Day" calendar hanging behind the cash register.

I said, "What's the date today?"

She looked at her watch. "Well, it's after midnight so I guess it's the fourth." She ripped the big "3" off the calendar.

"What's the word today?" I asked.

She got up close to it and said, "Lugubrious."

"Dismal or depressing," I said. She smiled at me and I knew I was right.

The cook in the back shouted out, "Sounds like something you don't want on your shoes."

I laughed at that. I reached into the inner pocket

of my jacket and found a creamy colored envelope. Inside was a letter on fancy letterhead that said "Saint Marjorie's Episcopal Cathedral." The salutation read, "Dear Rev. Dark."

"I'm an Episcopal priest," I said. I didn't mean to say it out loud. I was just surprised.

"'Scuse me?" she asked. Her name-tag said "Molly" but she didn't look like a Molly to me.

I scanned the letter. "I'm the new associate priest at Saint Marjorie's." I said, "I'm starting my new job today." The letter said I was expected on the fourth. I wondered what time they opened.

"I know that church," the man in the apron said as he put a hot steaming plate of pancakes on the counter. "You ever been there, Father?"

I shook my head. "I was assigned."

Molly placed the plate in front of me. The smell of them wafted up and filled my nose. I closed my eyes and inhaled deeply. Oh, I do love this place. When I opened them again, Molly and the cook were watching me. They must have thought I was praying or something. Guys in collars, they pray in restaurants.

I shoved a fork into the center of the stack and twirled it, scraping a hole about the size of a quarter. Then I filled the hole with the syrup from the cabin shaped jug on the counterthat was on the counter. I let the hole fill and pour down over the sides of the stack. Oh, lovely.

I shoved a fork full in my mouth and with my mouth still full I looked at the cook and said, "Thas wunnrful."

The big man behind the counter practically blushed. I guess he didn't get a lot of compliments. "Syrup is from a little town in Ohio. Guy named Leroy makes it in what's left of his grandfather's barn. Best you can get."

I believed him. With a mouthful I said, "Tell me about the church."

His smile faded. "Not a great neighborhood. Lotta drug problems. Used to be kinda nice down there."

I shoved another fork full of the fruity fluffy miracles in my mouth and closed my eyes.

An hour later I had eaten ten and was paying my bill with the cash that Gabriel had put in my wallet. The wallet itself had a cowboy on the front and looked like a grade schooler at summer camp had sewn it. I left a large tip. Molly gave me a huge cup of coffee for the road. As I was on my way out into the night, the cook—Dave was his name—came out into the lobby area. "Uh, Reverend? Father?"

I said, "Yes?" in my most holy voice. I had learned from the best.

He said, "I was wondering...I mean...I know this sounds silly...but could you bless my place? Do they do that in the Episcopal church?"

I honestly had no idea. I put my hand on the countertop and rubbed the wood with my palm. I closed my eyes and said, "God, bless this establishment. Keep it safe from danger and low tipping customers. Bless these your servants and give them strength and patience and hold a comfortable chair for them when they get to heaven. Amen."

I looked up. I wasn't sure if that was what they were wanting or not. Molly looked as though she might cry. Dave put his baseball cap back on backward and shook my hand. Molly grabbed me and hugged me so hard I thought she might break a rib. "Ohhhh, that was just so sweet." She said. "Especially that part about the comfortable chairs. Do you think that's what heaven is really like?"

I said, "They have a special section for waitresses. You get to sit back and let someone serve you for eternity. You're going to love it."

They laughed. They thought I was kidding.

* * *

I was just getting used to the whole driving thing again when I saw the light in my rear view mirror. It wasn't from a car behind me, but from my backseat. "Gabriel," I said.

"Reverend Dark," he answered.

"That's cute," I said, "making me a priest."

"Episcopal," he said, "not Catholic. Reverend or Father. Either one is correct."

"Episcopal means I can have sex, right?" I asked.

"The Episcopal church allows their priests to get married," he said. "You won't have time. Plus, you're not human. You can't get married."

"Archangels. Always with you and the rules."

"Someone has to do it," he said.

"You're no fun."

"Neither is my job."

I looked at him in the rear view mirror. He was

looking out the window at the city. I couldn't read his expression at all. He was right, though, it had to be rough. He was a glorified camp counselor, except that the campers can fly. How annoying would that be? When all the campers want to have fun, someone gets to be the hard ass. "Could you dim a little?" I asked. "Makes it hard to drive."

He dimmed and waited. "What? No joke about how bright Gabriel is? Or how many angels does it take to change the light bulb in Gabriel's butt?"

"I haven't heard that one," I said. "What's the answer?"

He ignored me. "I'm just here to give a quick warning. You have to play nice."

Yep, definitely a camp counselor. "Play nice?"

"I mean it this time."

"You said that last time."

The little bugger paused and looked at me in the mirror. "How were the pancakes?"

That was really low. He knew how much I loved the place. These senses. He also knew that I knew that he could make this all go away in a second and this would be my last assignment. Ever. He was the camp counselor with the list of parent phone numbers. Behave yourself or you lose your pudding cup before bed. It started to rain again and I hit the wipers. "Could you dim a little more please? You're reflecting in the rain."

The light in my backseat went out. I checked the mirror. He had left.

I was getting used to the skin now. My stomach felt full and happy, but there was still an emptiness that I couldn't figure out. I rolled the window down as I took the exit into the city. I smelled the night air. There wasn't a lot of traffic this time of night. I stopped at a traffic light. I saw a homeless man in a doorway trying to keep his feet out of the rain. A woman in a very short skirt and a lot of very red lipstick stepped off the curb and walked toward my car. She said, "Hey father, wanna go to heaven?"

I stepped on the gas without waiting for the light to change.

CHAPTER FOUR

A STAR OVER THE I (EYE)
A blog about nothing, written for no one in particular, by someone who pretty much stopped giving a rat's ass about things a long time ago.

ENTRY #657

Mom just came home from her meeting at the church and she's all aflutter. Apparently the diocese says we're getting a new minister to go with the old one...and get this...they want the new one to work with the youth.

There are no youth. There's enough little kids to make a nativity scene at Christmas and then there is me. I gave up playing Mary a long time ago. The last time I was Mary, I was 14 and towered over some sixth-grader playing Joseph. He kept holding my hand and smiling and saying that maybe we should go find a room in the inn. Kid is a perv. Yes, I know a perv when I see one, Dr. Conners.

Mom wanted me to know that this new guy wasn't a replacement for Rev. Haberkorn. I really like Rev. Haberkorn. I liked him a lot when I was a kid and he was the only one who didn't give me that judgmental look when I went through a...let's say a *phase* last year. He's a sweet old guy who looks like he's counting the days till he retires and moves to Florida or wherever it is old Episcopal priests go. Is there a, like, a home for them?

And yes, I go to church. This is me flipping the bird to those of you who seem to have a problem with that. I grew up in that that church. I think Rev. Haberkorn is probably one of the coolest old people I know, and he *doesn't judge*. I asked him once about how people in the church are a bunch of hypocritical gossips and he said, if Jesus Christ himself ever came into our church there would be someone there to tell him to get a haircut.

I want there to be a group house on the beach for retired clergy people. Kind of like a reality show, only *no cameras*. We'll just give you all kinds of stuff to have a great life and then we'll go away and let you have it.

Back in a sec, she who must be obeyed is screaming at me for something.

Okay, she wanted to tell me all about the new guy. His name is Michael Dark. I have to admit that's a cool name for a priest. Rev. Dark. (Although *Father* Dark would be much cooler. I wonder if he's open to a title bump?) He'll probably be one of those nerfy Oooo-I'm-all-spooky-and-good-with-young-people types. We had a youth minister before. I wasn't old enough to be in the group. There was something about drinking on a mission trip and then we didn't see him again.

I hate it when adults say "young people" like they are purposely not saying "teenager" and think teenagers appreciate that somehow. If I was talking to you and said, "You know, that Sunday school class where the *old people* are." Do you think they'd appreciate that? I'll try it on Sunday and let you know.

I just finished Googling Rev. Dark (God, I hope he has a tattoo) and he looks boring as hell. Google says he's originally from Akron. College in Ohio. Seminary in Chicago. (That might be fun.) There's a list of all his accomplishments, but nothing out of the ordinary. Really, really ordinary. So ordinary he makes me think that there's another layer there. Like maybe he *does* have a tattoo and it's of a seriously bloody Inquisition. Nah, won't happen. Rev. Michael Dark is probably as boring as most other ministers. Mom says he'll be here by next Sunday. That means word will get out and the entirety of the *old person* police/ judge/jury squad will be out in force and sitting in the back row to pass out looks of disappointment and stage whispers.

Last Easter I wore a brand new dress just to please my mother. White dress, heels, and I even cut back on the eye shadow. Happy Easter, Mom! We sat right in front of the back-row ladies and just before the prayer one of them leaned over to her white-gloved co-juror and whispered really loudly. "Who does she think she's fooling?"

No, I didn't turn around and flick something at her. Another gift to my mother. But I did sneak out a really offensive girl-fart and make us all sit in it for a few minutes. You're welcome, Jesus.

CHAPTER FIVE

I slept for a few hours in the backseat of my car. Note to self: Next time ask Gabriel for a van where one can stretch out a little. I woke up with the city. It was already starting to vibrate but had not yet worked itself up to a full buzz. I opened the car door and stood up to stretch. I was in Saint Marjorie's parking lot and there was a coffee shop called Java Joe's across the street. I think I will like working here. The air was cold and the wind blew through my black clergy shirt, but I didn't mind. I had removed the white collar and had tossed it into the front seat. Took me five minutes to figure out how it worked, but I managed to get it off. Getting it back on seemed harder. I grabbed the jacket that I had used as a blanket and put it on. Looking at myself in the mirror, I saw I was a wrinkled mess. I combed my hair with my fingers. I looked like a very frumpy priest. I found a pair of eyeglasses in the jacket pocket and put them on. For show. Not for vision.

I opened the trunk and found two huge suitcases. Note to self: Next time put the suitcases in the backseat and sleep in the trunk. One of the suitcases had a side pocket full of bathroom articles. I thanked Gabriel for the attention to detail, but not out loud. Wouldn't want him to get a swelled head or anything. I found a leather pouch with a shaving kit, put all the things I needed into it, then walked across the street to Java Joe's. The sign said "Open." My watch said six o'clock. I went inside and found a men's room. In a few minutes I emerged shaven and combed. I looked less tired, but just as frumpy. I sat at the counter.

"Get you something, Father?" I hadn't noticed the man when I came in—perhaps because I might have mistaken him for the refrigerator. The mountain of a human smiled at me. His arms were covered in military tattoos, now somewhat faded and considerably less detailed then they once were. I could also tell by the way he spoke to me that he had lost most or all of his hearing.

I used the American Sign Language I remembered and signed, "Coffee, please."

He smiled. It was a good smile. "It's okay," he said. "I can read lips just fine."

I said it out loud this time adding the words "Very," "Very," and "Large," in that order. He disappeared behind the counter and returned with a cup that could have been used as a cereal bowl. "Are you the new priest at Saint Madge's?"

I must have given him a look because he immediately said, "Sorry, I mean Saint Marjorie's."

I laughed. "It's okay. Is Saint Madge's what they call it around here?"

He nodded as he filled the soup basin in front of me. I took a drink and felt the warmth from the tips of my fingers to the ends of my hair. I sighed heavily. He smiled and offered his hand. "Dwight."

I shook it. "Michael." Then added, "Dwight, I have a feeling that you and I may be seeing a lot of each other."

The morning vibration of the city increased, and more and more headlights could be seen on the street. More and more people filed in and out of the coffee shop. Dwight became a machine. Every move was well practiced. He knew who was coming and what they would be drinking. Trays were filled. Cups were stacked. Orders were taken, and Dwight did it all by himself. Most people who came in waved instead of just saying "Good morning." I was amazed at how many ordinary Philadelphians knew the sign for coffee. Dwight didn't stop. Not for three hours. I watched him the whole time. I left the counter only once because, like I said, it was a really big cup of coffee.

When things started to wind down and there were fewer than five customers in the room, Dwight looked at me and said, "That's ninety percent of my day, right there."

I shook my head in amazement.

"People will come in for a bagel at lunch, but I'll be closed up by 3:00."

"What's the neighborhood like?" I asked when I had his attention.

"Don't go out at night," he said. "Least not too late. Lotta bums in the area...'scuse me, Father...lotta homeless folks. They're out during the day. Once you get to midnight or so, all the gangs come out. The drug dealers and the pimps. It's like they live under the street and just come up through the sewer. You know what I mean?"

I nodded. I knew exactly what he meant. All too well. I'll tell you about that later too. I said, "You must get in here about four. Aren't you worried?"

He stood up to his full height and crossed his cannon-like arms over his battleship chest. "Oh yeah," I said.

He caught me looking out at the church across the street and said, "Saint Marjorie's is a grand old lady. She's the oldest building on the block. Used to be the nice neighborhood around her. Now all the rich folks come in on Sunday morning and are back in their homes by noon. They don't come down this part of town during the week."

"Does the church have any sort of outreach program in the neighborhood?" I asked.

Dwight wrinkled his nose like he had smelled something disgusting. "Nah. Not unless you count the rummage sale."

I raised my eyebrows at him questioningly.

He sort of laughed. "Once a year all the members bring in last year's mink coats and their old Armani suits and they have a huge sale. 'Cept none of the members will actually shop at the sale 'cause they don't want to be seen buying some other member's mink. The homeless, they come out of the woodwork, and you get these bag ladies struttin' around like they're royalty. It's a sight to see."

"The kingdom of God," I said, but I wasn't facing him. I still had hours before I was supposed to meet my new boss, so I took a seat and watched my new city come alive. People came in and out. Dwight had bags of gooey chocolate things made up. Some folks came in with the well-practiced ease of grabbing a bag, filling their own coffee, and dropping a few bills on the counter.

Hundreds of people passed by the window moving at a pace that I hadn't seen in years. Where did these people have to go?

I sipped my coffee and thought about what Gabriel had said about being good this time. All I could think was, "I will if they will."

CHAPTER SIX

A STAR OVER THE I (EYE)
A blog about nothing, written for no one in particular,
by someone who pretty much stopped giving a rat's
ass about things a long time ago.

ENTRY #659
You do have to hand it to Rev. Haberkorn. I told you
he was the only one who didn't seem to judge me
when I had that...uh...trouble last year. The man actually called and asked me if I would be willing to come
to church and set up the new computer for the new
associate. Somebody cue up "Isn't it ironic?".

Mom says she'll drive me into town tomorrow. Rev.
Haberkorn says that's okay because the new priest
drove all night to get here and will probably be settling
into the new digs and getting acquainted with the city.

Long time ago St Marjorie's used to be a seminary.
The top two floors were dorm rooms. Then one year
they decided to make them into apartments and took
out the floor-slash-ceiling between the two and left six
or eight apartments with really high ceilings. I grew up

in the church. I know every inch. Snuck into those apartments a few years ago. Wish I lived there. Rev. Haberkorn has his own place outside of town.

Wonder if that's a good trade-off. "Here, we'll give you a great place to live. High ceilings, full kitchen, nice bedroom with a balcony...no charge. The only catch is you have to live above your job." Mom says Dad used to live at his job.

So I'm reading up on installations and heading into the church tomorrow for some install work. I'm thinking of putting a virus in the secretary's computer so that every time she types the word "as" it will add an extra "s" on the end. Is that wrong? Don't they make those people sign some sort of confidentiality oath or something? There was stuff said around that church that could only have come from the inside, and like I said, Rev. Haberkorn is awesome and I trust him.

CHAPTER SEVEN

Later that night...

Micah's bare feet settled in the dust on each step as he made his way to the roof of the cathedral. The thick black leather coat was longer than his cassock, and he had to gather it up and hold it in front of him to keep from tripping on it. The door at the top of the musty stairwell was locked but his shiny new master key opened it easily. He stepped out onto the roof. The air was cold and it wasn't raining but he knew that if he stood there long enough the mist would collect on his glasses. He removed them and slid them into a coat pocket. He put the key in the other one.

He stared up at the two remaining gargoyles. At one time there had been more than a dozen around the outside of the building, but wind and rain and age had damaged them as wind and rain and age will do to any building.

The first was a squat little fellow with a large belly and enormous eyes. He squatted with this hands resting between his feet. His head was point-

ed down, studying the street, as if he was weighing the pros and cons of on whom he should pounce.

The second held on to the building with one massive stone hand. His body leaned out over the city as if he was quite comfortable with heights. Stare at it for any length of time, and you would think that perhaps this demon had been scampering up the side of the cathedral and stopped here by the balcony to rest a moment before continuing up over the edge of the roof and into your nightmares.

From his hanging position, the gargoyle eyed with piercing suspicion Micah and anyone who came out onto the large outdoor balcony. Of the two stone silent guards, it was this one who made folks the more uncomfortable. Even property manager Jack did not like to come out onto this balcony, and only did so in the daylight and even then made very sure not to look up at the creature he knew was looking down at him.

"Hello, boys," Micah said. He expected no response and got none. Placing his hands on the ledge of the stone balcony he looked down the five stories to the street below. He inhaled deeply through his nose and smelled the night. No, not the night. He smelled the dark. Dark smelled the same now as it always had. Night smelled of exhaust fumes, neon gas, winos' urine, cheap perfume, cooking meat, and baking bread. It smelled of the steam coming up through the grates and cooking whatever had been spilled on them during the day. Darkness had a fragrance all its own. The smell of dark hadn't changed in two thousand years.

He took another deep breath and allowed it to happen to him once again. He watched as his hands doubled in size. The skin became a dark leathery gray. The backs of his hands sprouted hair that continued up his arm under the sleeve of the black coat. He felt the increase in his chest. He felt his shoulders expand to fill the coat. His legs grew and widened. The coat, which had hung past his feet, now reached to just behind his knees. His knees looked as though they had grown an extra kneecap so that he could bend them in either direction. His feet grew in proportion to the legs and a new odd-looking toe protruded out the back of his heel. It had a long gray nail on the top that curved around on itself. This extra toe would allow him to perch on small ledges and the edges of rooftops.

The muscles in his face pushed forward from his nose to his chin. His hair both grew and shrunk at the same time. His graying blonde pastor's cut was replaced by a Mohawk of absolute ebony. It hung down over his forehead and the back of his neck. Each individual strand measured more than two feet. He used his giant gray mallet of a hand to push the mane of black to one side.

He bent forward. The wings were always the only painful part of the transformation. Micah never knew why, and he certainly wasn't going to ask anyone. The pain ripped through his back as the wings pushed through his skin and out through the holes in the back of the coat. The wings unfolded themselves into a cape that was larger than he was. The feathers were coarse and dark like those *of a raven or a crow. He did once ask Gabriel about the feathers. Wouldn't something more akin to bat wings be more appropriate?*

Gabriel had smirked at him and made some comment under his breath about fashion critics.

Micah—no longer was even a piece of him Michael—stood up on the ledge and stretched his arms. He balled himself up like a child doing a well-practiced cannonball. He dropped into the night like a black stone dropping into a deep dank well. He unfolded himself at the last moment and waited for the first scream.

It was a man of about fifty who was just coming out of a bar. The scream was high-pitched and girl-ish and tomorrow he would simply tell himself that a bat had come too close to his face; that it was only a trick of perspective and in his condition he only thought he saw...something else.

The current caught Micah's wings and lifted him a few feet above the traffic. The screams then came from both sides of the street at once. It was as if he rode on the waves of their fear and shock. He lifted himself back into the night, higher up than the streetlights could illuminate him. He came to rest on another section of the cathedral roof. He was clutching the edge of the bell tower with his six toes.

Micah laughed. He felt whole again.

* * *

Dontay didn't feel the cold anymore. The drug had done its work already. Even if he didn't get completely stoned tonight, he could at least feel the warmth inside him for a little while. He held the crack-laden cigarette to his lips and inhaled deeply. The nerve endings in his body began to fire up and pop like he had injected some of the exploding candy he had when he was a kid. Dontay was 15. His senses came alive. He felt as though he could tell the weight of the cigarette down to the decimal point. His tongue felt like he could taste the number of grains of salt on the pretzels that he smelled from what he was sure was blocks away.

Only briefly did the memory of what he would feel like in the morning slide past his brain. It was there like a photograph, and then with no effort he was able to push it aside and think of nothing...only feel the world around him. What was it that ancient priest had said? "Let tomorrow worry about tomorrow." He decided he would worry about emptiness tomorrow. Tonight he was warm. Tonight he could feel the threads around the hole in his sock.

He leaned back against the building, feeling every tiny bump of the bricks through his too thin jacket. He exhaled through his nose, breathing out twin plumes of smoke. He closed his eyes. Even if he had kept them open, it would have made no difference. Even with his false sense of heightened senses, he never would have seen or heard the giant walk up on him.

He felt warm air on his skin, but the smell was

putrid. It was a sour sort of vomit smell combined with cooking flesh. Dontay had watched the members of a street gang burn a man alive, once about two years before, and had never been able to get the smell out of his nose. Sometimes it came back to him when his grandmother was cooking dinner. This smell...this smell that was invading his pleasure was a thousand times worse.

He opened his eyes, and immediately his bladder let go. The black face was that of a horse...or maybe a lizard...or maybe both. The eyes that met his were so yellow that Dontay wondered if there were any pupils in them at all. He opened his mouth to scream, but all that came out was the quietest "ahh." He was suddenly overwhelmed with the fear that this "ahh" would be his last sound ever.

The hand came out of nowhere, and the fingers wrapped themselves around his shirtfront. He was suddenly lifted three feet off the ground. The black thing did this with no more effort than Dontay had used to hold his baby sister's doll above her head. The warmth had left him now. Even the urine that dampened his leg felt like ice water. He had never felt so cold...so empty...so suddenly. The black thing looked from Dontay's eyes to Dontay's right hand. Dontay followed its gaze. His elbow was still bent. His hand still held the cigarette between two fingers. He had frozen like a statue when the thing had grabbed him and only now was he aware that he hadn't moved.

With its other hand, the thing reached and took

the cigarette from Dontay. It held the cigarette up in front of the young man's face and waited for him to focus on it. Dontay thought that the fingers of that massive hand looked like the sausage his grandmother cooked for dinner sometimes. The cherry-red ash that graced the tip of the cigarette didn't get any brighter but it burned its way down to the black things fingers and then vanished in smoke. It happened in about two seconds.

Dontay found his voice.

"Oh, jesus...jesus...jesus...jesus...jesus...jesus... jesus...jesus...jesus." Dontay repeated over and over, unaware that he was even speaking. The black thing placed a finger the size of cigar on his lips, stopping the words.

"He's not here," the black thing said. "He doesn't like the big city, but I'll tell him you asked about him." The voice was so deep that Dontay felt the rumble in his stomach like the bass on his friend Darrell's stereo.

"Why would you want to do this?" the thing asked. It reached into his front pocket and pulled out the small plastic bag. Three small white rocks. Fifty dollars worth of mind-numbing sense-enhancing crystal gleamed out, the whitest thing in Dontay's field of vision. Pinched between the thumb and forefinger of the giant paw, Dontay watched helplessly as it too went up with a silent poof.

The black thing leaned its head back and studied Dontay's face. It looked to him like the thing was studying him the way an artist would study a lump of clay. It was appraising him.

"N-*n-n-n-n-n-n-n-n-n-no-no-no-no-no*. No. No. No," *Dontay said. But it was a whisper so faint he doubted the black thing heard him. He closed his eyes. He became aware of the smell of burning hair. He felt a mild warmth on his chin, and he realized the black thing was burning the patch of hair under his lip. The one his grandmother hated. The one he had been so proud to grow when most of his friends could not. It was burning off his hair with its thumb.*

The thing studied its work. "Better," *it said.*

Then it leaned in close to Dontay's ear. Dontay could smell the vile stench again. He nearly threw up.

"I could have killed you," *the thing said. Dontay thought of the way the plastic bag had melted in its fingers.*

"You won't do that again," *the thing said. It did not say it as threat. It didn't ask it as a question. It merely said it as a statement of fact, the way one might say the sky was blue or water is wet.*

"No. *n-n-n-n-n-n-n-n-n-no*," *Dontay managed to say again. This time he was agreeing with it. He felt the grip on his shirt relax. He felt the concrete under his shoes again. It was then he realized how large the thing was. It was then he realized the burning smell from before also included his shirt-front.*

The black things took one step backward and became part of the shadow.

Dontay fainted.

CHAPTER EIGHT

A STAR OVER THE I (EYE)
A blog about nothing, written for no one in particular,
by someone who pretty much stopped giving a rat's
ass about things a long time ago.

ENTRY #660

Holy shit, you should see the news. Apparently a giant flying gorilla-like monster attacked the good people of downtown Philadelphia last night. Saw the report, and some of the eye witnesses are right downtown near the church.

Mom says she doesn't want to drive me in today because it might not be safe. I tell her it's okay, whatever it was seems to come out at night. Then she says she doesn't want to drive me in 'cause the traffic will be really bad with gawkers driving in to see what's going on. I tell her that Rev. Haberkorn himself called me and asked for my help in setting things up for the new priest. I give her the sad-girl eyes and make her think that joining a church group might do me some good after all that's happened, and she relents. We're going in this afternoon. She's going to work and I'm supposed to walk to grab the bus outside of St Madge's and come to the hospital. It will be late and Mom says I can use the computer at the nurses' station to do homework or sleep in one of the extra beds. Don't make that face, I do it all the time.

Giant scary monster with wings.

Cooooooooooool.

CHAPTER NINE

It feels like a hangover. That's just for the record. Just so you know. You wake up from a "night on the town" and it feels like a hangover. My head felt like a pumpkin that someone had scraped the insides out of. I sometimes wondered what other guardians felt like when they woke up in the morning. Did they feel like this? Did they wake up and feel like fresh sheets on a clothesline and their breath smelling of strawberries? I wasn't like other guardians. I got in on a technicality and they just have to deal with me. For all his faults, Gabriel recognizes my unique gifts. Somebody gets the shitty jobs. Somebody has to. Sometimes, some people deserve them.

My apartment was huge. I was on the fourth floor of the cathedral. The fifth floor was mostly empty except for storage. The apartment had two massive bedrooms and a living room with a high ceiling. The way it was explained to me yesterday was that about a hundred years ago the top floors of the cathedral were used as dorm rooms for student priests. Somewhere in the fifties, the place was renovated and the fourth floor became apartments and the fifth floor became storage. A floor was removed, making a high ceiling with large windows overlooking the city. Kind of ironic that the renovation bricked up the windows but left the balconies. The senior priest got himself a big house in the suburbs, and the associate—yours truly—got the apartment. It was nicer than anything I could have found in the city, and the only drawback was that I lived above my job.

My boss is the Rev. Dr. Lucas Haberkorn. Nice guy. He's got old eyes, you know the kind. Granted the man is seventy-something, but he's got an old soul. Moves kinda slow, got those cute little tuffets of white hair above his ears, but he's got eyes that say, "Sit down, Sonny. You're not going to show me anything new."

I met Haberkorn yesterday. When I told him I slept in my car, he practically gave me the day off. Gave me a tour. Shook my hand and told me to move my stuff in and get some sleep, we'd meet tomorrow for the formal stuff. Must be nice to be in charge. Jack, the property manager, said that Haberkorn had done two tours in Vietnam as an army chaplain. He came home and did twenty years with the Philadelphia fire department, emergency work and rescue. The diocese likes to reward guys like this. When he hit sixty they assigned him to Saint Marjorie's, thinking he'd retire and go away by sixty-five. He was in his seventies now. You must admire a guy who sees it through to the end.

Saint Marjorie's has a huge endowment (i.e., money that does nothing else but makes more money). Saint Marjorie's could operate forever and never have to hold another service. Rev. Haberkorn gets to do weddings, funerals, baptisms, and Sunday morning services. He's never had to worry about money. All of the "God" and none of the garbage. A parish minister's dream.

I guess it goes without saying that I didn't get a lot of sleep last night either, but at least what I got was in a bed and I didn't have a seatbelt digging into my back. I don't know what your own bed comes equipped with, but mine? No seat belts. Angels don't need sleep. Gabriel can just go right on being annoying 24/7. Then again, time is different in heaven, so technically...never mind. Guardians do need sleep. But when you work the night shift, so to speak, you tend to get a hangover as I already mentioned.

I checked the baggage. No aspirin. Thanks, Gabriel. You can remember the toothpaste with the whitener, but you can't remember the Tylenol. I checked the bathroom. There was one—count them—*one* Advil sitting on the shelf in the medicine cabinet. I swallowed it. Wow. Zip-a-dee-do-da, what's next?

I padded into the living room in my socks and boxers. I'd left my coat on the back of the sofa. I picked it up and draped it over my arm like a quilt. It was exactly what you would want to find in your new associate pastor's apartment: a long black leather coat twice his size with two holes cut in the back. You want to see how fast a rumor mill works? Just let something like that slip in a church.

The Ladies' Friendly Society had filled my kitchen cupboards with the basics. Ever heard of the Lades' Friendly Society? They're a group of older women who hang out in Episcopal churches and help get things done. They feed the homeless, hold rummage sales, and scare small children. Okay, I made the last part up. They're ladies who have made the church their second home and like most of us, can be kind of picky about who they let in.

I asked Jack about the LFS and he said—and this is his quote—"The Ladies' Friendly Society is neither." I kind of like Jack. He said that most of the time the church doesn't need a security system because the LSF pretty much knows who's coming and going at all times. He said there was a back entrance where I could come and go without having to use the front door. So far, my private balcony was working pretty well for me.

In the center cupboard I found coffee. God bless the LSF. There was a coffee maker on the counter. I read the directions to see if making coffee was any different since the last time I was here. I lost count of how many scoops I had used and rather than try and dump the coffee back in the bag I simply started counting again. Like I said, it feels like a hangover.

I thought maybe I would go and visit my new friend Dwight, but I had visited my new friend

Dwight three times yesterday and I thought people might start to talk.

I opened the freezer and found a variety of fruity-doughy things that fit in a toaster. There was a toaster on the counter and I dropped one of the fruity-doughy things in the slot and pushed the button.

Poured some coffee and the toaster popped. The fruity-doughy thing was still frozen. I put my hand on the top of the toaster and felt nothing. I dunked my red fruity doughy thing in my coffee and ate it standing over the sink. I think it was raspberry. It was red anyway. Tasted red. I decided that my one visit to Dwight would be this morning.

I found a radio and a list the LSF had written down of all the wholesome family Christian stations in the area and their place on the dial. I don't know how it works where you're from, but around here it's like all the Christian stations are crammed down at the end of the dial below 90. The upper end of the dial above 107 is usually where you'll find the music that guys in long black leather coats listen to.

I turned on the radio and winced as Monica Sunnydale's "Son Beam" pierced my temple like a railroad spike. One tap of the SEEK button, and I caught the opening bars of "Teenage Wasteland." (Yes, I know the real name of the song is "Bubba O'Riley" but everybody calls it "Teenage Wasteland." You purists make me sick. And you think you can make fun of Trekkies, c'mon.) I turned it up and bounced around the apartment, allowing Mr. Townsend and Mr. Daltrey to heal my aching head. (No offense to Mr. Jesus, and I'm sure he would tell me if he was actually offended. We have that kind of relationship.)

I showered and changed into my priestly clothes. In the suitcase that Gabriel had provided I found six (count them, *six*) pairs of Converse All-stars. I thought, "Shit, they're going to make me work with teenagers."

I slipped on a pair of solid black ones, hoping they wouldn't look too unprofessional.

Dwight was in good spirits when I went in. The morning rush had cleaned out the muffin bin, much to my disappointment, but Dwight produced a paper bag with Fr. Dark written in classic black Sharpie marker on the side. "Knew you'd be in. I saved you one."

I made the sign of the cross over him and he smiled. I guess some people think that's pretty cool. I wonder if they think it wears off and I have to do it again.

I told him I had an appointment and had to go. He put a lid on a cup of coffee. I paid and was out the door to explore my new city in the daylight hours. It was cold and I had on a thick yuppie cat-alog jacket over my clergy shirt. On the crowded street, people parted and gave me the right of way. I guess they were afraid I was going to jump them and make them say the Lord's Prayer.

The streets were wet and the crowds were thick. Where I come from there were no buildings over two stories tall and you could see the sky no matter where you were. Not here. Here it was like you could feel life beneath the street and above in the offices where work never seemed to stop. The city hummed, all the time. It never stopped.

After about six blocks I crossed the street. I was still far away from Philadelphia's historical district and decided to save the Liberty Bell for another day. A woman in a traffic cop's orange vest stopped a bus for me. I could get used to this. I crossed the street and passed the alley where I had met the young man the night before. I felt a small twinge of guilt. I had, after all, made the young man piss himself, but at least he would remember. I bought a paper. It was probably too soon to expect a write-up on a "giant demon" or "night creature" but I looked anyway. Nothing. I heard a voice say, "Hey Father."

I turned and saw the young woman in the short skirt and red lips. I guess she had the day shift today.

She smiled.

I smiled.

She took a step toward me.

I walked the other way. Yeah, yeah, all God's children, I know. I know what you're thinking and you probably know what I was thinking but I have several bosses and not one of them would be happy to see me passing the time of day with a short skirt and red lips. Maybe she just wanted a bite of my muffin.

When I arrived back at Saint Marjorie's, Alice was there. Alice was a pudding of a woman who seemed to have penciled her eyebrows into a permanent look of disapproval.

I said, "Good morning, Alice."

She said, "I think you and I need to have a talk about the In-Out board."

She pointed a red painted fingernail at a white marker board beside her desk. On it was an intricate graph with the names of all staff members and a system of magnetic colored dots that seemed to indicate who was in and who was out. That was the beginning of our relationship. You don't mess with church secretaries. Another reason for the lack of a good security system is that you have a secretary who can fix you with a stare that would make just about anybody who didn't belong there turn around and walk back out the door. You really don't want to mess with church secretaries...or demon-possessed people. Church secretaries and demon-possessed people give me the willies.

She fixed me with a stare. I said, "I brought you a good-morning muffin."

CHAPTER TEN

Sitting across the desk from Rev. Haberkorn, I could not stop looking at those eyes. Everything about his body language said "tired"—everything about those eyes said "servant."

I was guessing that at one time, God said, "Whom shall I send?" and Lucas Haberkorn said, "Ooo, Ooo, pick me! Pick me!" And God took him at his word.

He said, "I'm giving you the 7am service." I tried not to flinch but he caught it anyway. "I'm old and I'm in charge." He smiled. "You'll assist me at the 9 and 11."

I nodded.

"You'll also be in charge of the youth group."

What I was thinking was, "I hate you, Gabriel," but what I said was, "How large is the youth group?"

He said, "We're starting it today. Been advertising it for weeks. Kids will be able to come in after school and do their homework and play Ping-Pong or whatever."

"Ping-Pong," I thought.

"Staff meetings are on Tuesdays," Haberkorn continued. "Dorothy McConnell is our education director. You'll meet her tomorrow. She may ask you to lead the children's chapel. Do you like working with the little ones?"

What I thought was, "I hate you, Gabriel." What I said was, "I love it."

He smiled. "Neither do I." Can't put anything over on this guy. "God gives us all gifts," he said. "Dorothy's is children. Mine is golf."

I smiled.

"Do you golf?" he asked.

"Never," I told him. "I play a mean racquetball." I chose something I thought he would never ask to join me in.

"Too fast for me," he said. "I like golf. You don't run. You ride around in a cart and you enjoy the sunshine. I'll have to teach you."

"I'd like that," I said. The truth is that I would. I could imagine that this man had some great stories, and I would be a new set of ears that hadn't heard any of them.

"Well," he said, in a tone that meant "meeting over."

He stood.

I stood.

He shook my hand. "Look, Michael, when I got the letter from the bishop asking if I would give you a shot...after what happened in Cleveland, I almost said no."

I nodded. I should probably ask Gabriel about that.

"But I worship a God of second chances," Haberkorn said. "So we took you on. Nobody else knows about the letter."

I tried to look grateful. "I appreciate it, Lucas. Truly I do. I won't let you down."

"Good," he said as if it was all over and I'm sure that it was...whatever it has been in the first place. He said, "I'm sure Alice has a nice big stack of forms for you to fill out."

"About Alice," I said. "Office manager? Receptionist? Personal assistant? What's the proper term?"

"Office manager," he said. "Don't ever use the word 'secretary,' but don't forget flowers on Secretaries' Day."

"Got it."

"Do you have plans for lunch?"

"No," I said. "I've never had an authentic Philly cheese steak. I thought I'd start my own research on who has the best."

"I know a place," he said. "Join me? 12:30."

I smiled and he gently ushered me to the door. I've been fighting for a very long time, and this man with his gentle way just led me out of the room like it was my idea. Alice was in the hallway waiting. She had a file in her hand as thick as a history text-book.

She waved it at me. "Taxes. Insurance. Credit cards. Tax exemption forms. And your youth group budget." She handed me the file and turned to leave.

"No secret handshake?" I asked.

She went back to her desk without sharing one.

* * *

Rev. Haberkorn took me to the Reading Terminal Market. I've been back dirt-side many times over the years and I can tell you this is the closest anyone has come to what the markets in Jerusalem were like. The Terminal Market is dark. Even if you are close to the windows you're still in the shade of the bridge, but you'd swear you were outside. The people are crowded in bumping and jostling each other. There's fresh produce and things baking everywhere. And, oh, the smells, cooking meat, and pastry, and pretzels, and thick wedges of citrus fruits. There are trays with live crabs, and people shouting in foreign languages. People are selling books and toys and pottery. I stood for a while and watched two Amish girls make pretzels. Seriously, it was entertaining as hell. They'd roll out the dough into a snake and then with one fluid motion flip it into the shape we all know and love. Rev. Haberkorn bought two hot pretzels and handed me one. I could feel the hot butter seeping through the napkin. He said, "You need one of these because the line for cheese steaks is usually pretty long."

He was right, but we didn't care. We had pretzels. As we stood in line I became enraptured by the rhythm of the metal spatula as it clanged turning the onions. I heard the hiss of grease as the meat hit the tray. Peppers glowed. Cheese melted. From somewhere in the back of the giant hall I heard a piano. It was out of tune and the player wasn't all that talented but I didn't care. The song was "Come Thou Fount Of Every Blessing," and I thought, "How appropriate."

For a moment (and just for a moment), I really pitied Gabriel. He never allowed himself to be human. He never took on a dirt-side assignment himself. He always sent a guardian. I couldn't help but think that if he just took one assignment himself and got a little dirt on that white robe of his, he might loosen up a little. On the air, behind a whiff of strawberries, I caught the scent of strong coffee. I mentioned this to Haberkorn and he pointed to a place off to the right of where we were. It was one guy standing by six huge coffee makers that looked like they were made from ballistic missile casings. I made a promise to stop there before we left.

"I used to come here at two o'clock in the morning," he said. "It was still pretty crowded but with a different...uh...."

"Clientele?" I offered.

He nodded. I knew exactly what he meant. Some of my best friends were of a different clientele. "Why'd you quit?"

"I got old," he said disappointedly. "My doctor said to lay off the cheese steaks three times a week, and the neighborhood went downhill. It got safer to stay home and watch Johnny Carson with a bowl of cereal."

"Can't be the same atmosphere, though," I said.

He smiled. "You're young. You should get out in the city at night. Just be careful."

I said, "I'd love to do a little exploring." From the next booth over I heard someone shout several rapid-fire profanities in Hebrew. That *really* took me back. Oh yes, I could definitely get used to this city.

CHAPTER ELEVEN

A STAR OVER THE I (EYE)
A blog about nothing, written for no one in particular,
by someone who pretty much stopped giving a rat's
ass about things a long time ago.

ENTRY #661

Ooooo, the new priest is in the how-ouse. That looks lame when you write it oww-ut like tha-at. Father Dark is somewhere in the building. This was explained to me by the church secretary who appears to have the Sears Tower shoved up her butt. I told her why I was here, and she glared at me like I had peed on her carpet. I told her that Rev. Haberkorn had asked me to come in and install Rev. Michael's computer and software so it would be ready when he got to his office.

She told me I was late. I asked her if Rev. Michael had already been to his office. She said that he was in a meeting. I told her that it wouldn't take long and Rev. Haberkorn really wanted the new priest to feel like he was welcome. She told me what floor the office was on and that I should be as quick as possible.

It was an easy install. Nice computer. Some boring Bible software. Not hard at all. I'm also blogging from his office chair. Shhhhhh, don't tell Madame Pleasantry in the front office.

St. Madge's is a great place. There are these awesome gargoyles on the roof. (I think the secretary goes up there and practices her stare.) Like I said, I grew up here. I know the building and where all the skeletons and the keys are hidden.

Every time I hear the elevator door "ding," I listen for the feet. If it sounds like high heels, I'm going to crawl under the desk and pretend I'm doing something intricate. If it sounds like flat-soled clergy shoes, then I'm going to sit my ass right here in his chair and see what he does.

CHAPTER TWELVE

At three o'clock I was in my apartment review-
ing some books on how to minister to teenagers. I
thought not killing them was pretty good advice.
Several books recommended breaking larger
groups into smaller groups and planning various
things for them to do, then letting them switch
groups. Seemed logical. I had searched the church's
library (term used loosely) for books on how to
lead an Episcopal service. I had a feeling I was
going to be cramming. Then I remember that three
o'clock was when I was supposed to begin. Way to
start off my new job.

I arrived at my office to find a teenage girl sitting
in my chair, behind my desk, tapping away at my
computer. She turned and looked at me when I
came in.

She said, "Hey." (Teenagers, always with the for-
malities.)

I said, "I'm Reverend Dark."

She said, "Good, 'cause you just came in his
office without knocking."

"And you would be?"

"I would be Padi. That's with a *d* and not two *t*'s, and a star over the *i*."

"Padi. No *t*'s. Got it. And what, Padi with a *d*, are you doing on my computer?"

"Upgrading you."

I wasn't a big computer guy. The last time I actually used a computer, it was the size of a room and all it did was play Pong, but I assumed that her upgrading was a kind gesture.

I took a seat across from my own desk as she tapped away. "Are you part of the youth group?" I asked.

"Kinda," she said. "I *am* the youth group."

"That's going to make breaking the group into smaller groups of five or more a little difficult."

My computer made a sound like a horse breaking wind and went blank. She spun around in my chair and rested her arms on my desk and said, "I gave it sounds."

"That's very kind," I said.

"It will play the opening bars of 'Amazing Grace' when it starts up again."

"Can you make it play the opening bars of 'Imagine'?"

She looked surprised. "You didn't strike me as a John Lennon guy."

"You've known me for about 30 seconds," I said.

"Yeah," she motioned to the computer, "but I read your bio."

"Ah," I said, suddenly worried that she actually knew more about Michael Dark than I did. "Those things are padded."

"It said you excelled at creative worship practices."

I said, "That means I once set the sanctuary on fire."

She said, "Is that when you were in Cleveland?"

I nodded. I had to get a look at that bio. "Rev. Haberkorn said they'd been advertising the new youth group for months."

"Yeah, advertising it *here*," she said. "It's not like they actually want actual people from the neighborhood to show up."

"You showed up," I said.

"My mother thinks I spend too much time in front of the computer."

"Good thing you're getting involved in the church."

She nodded. A picture of Jesus surfing illuminated the screen. She didn't turn her head but I could tell she was waiting for my reaction. I impressed her by having none. The familiar bars of "Amazing Grace" drifted from the speakers.

"I boosted your sound board," she said. "And I got you the latest Word Pro. Yours was two years old."

"Advancements in technology will never cease."

"If you should happen to get an email from someone named Gorgone360, just tell them that the patch worked."

"Got it," I said, having no clue what anything in

that sentence meant. Is it likely that I will hear from Mr. Gorgon?"

She looked a little nervous. "Any of those programs are available on the Web," she said. "If you want more, ask me, okay? Don't ask Gorgon directly."

I nodded. I tried to look like we were sharing a secret.

She looked at me across my own desk like she owned it. "So," she said. "What's the plan for the youth group? Start a soccer team? Change the world? Study groups?"

I smiled. "You'd be surprised how much one person can change the world."

"Nice with the Jesus." She said.

I hadn't actually meant Jesus but I made a mental note to mention to him that his name had become an eponym.

"Reverend Dark?" a voice behind me said.

I stood and there in my doorway was an older black woman. She had put on her Sunday go-to-church-gloves on a Tuesday afternoon. She was quite short and she shifted from foot to foot as if one or the other was giving her trouble.

"Yes," I said in my most priestly voice, "what can I do for you?"

"My name is Roberta. I've been attending Saint Marjorie's for sixty-five years."

I smiled. Lifelong dedication impressed me. I took her gloved hand in both of mine, and she sandwiched mine with her other one. "Miss Roberta, I am delighted to meet you. Perhaps I can impose on you to give me a history of the church one of these days."

She beamed. "I would love to, but I have Book Club meeting down the street. I wanted to come and meet the new priest, and I wanted to enroll my grandson in your youth program."

"We'd love to have him," I said. I couldn't wait to tell them at tomorrow's staff meeting that the enrollment of the youth group had doubled. "We're here every day after school," I said. "Bring him by any time."

She looked off to the side of my door and made a come here motion.

"He's already here," she said. And with that she reached out and swatted someone with her gloved hand.

Around the corner stepped a young man who was taller than she was but still not my height. He had his hands shoved into his pockets and his head tilted to the side as if he was just too tired to hold it up.

Until yesterday he had sported a fine little soul patch beneath his lip. I had burned it off last night.

"This is my grandson, Dontay," she said.

"Pleased to meet you, Dontay." I reached out my hand and he shook it as if we had never met.

CHAPTER THIRTEEN

Later that night...

Micah stood on the ledge. He was barefoot again. The heavy coat weighed down on his shoulders. The coat was far too big for this form, yet he felt like this existence, this human shell was like wearing a coat that was way too small. He remembered what it was like to be human. He remembered the smell of a woman's hair, the sweat of a brother, the song his mother sang. He had all these memories of his own, and yet these days he only felt truly alive when he was no longer human.

A November wind blew up from the pavement and brought the smells of the city. It was an icy wind that barely moved the heavy leather trench coat he was wearing. The coat seemed to catch the wind and swirl it around his legs and torso. He felt the wind bite into him. He felt the cold in his bones. He had never known this kind of cold when he was alive. He had never seen the ocean or understood that the moon was something you could walk on.

It was like he had grown up inside a box and was released when he died. Now, he felt that claustrophobic feeling again. He wanted out. IT wanted out.

He spread his arms like cross and closed his eyes. He fell forward and felt the change begin before his feet left the concrete ledge. His face shifted. His hair sprouted. His bones expanded inside his thickening skin as the wind rushed through the black Mohawk and across his ears. The roar of the wind was deafening. He shouted to cover the noise.

He was still shouting at twenty feet from the pavement. At six feet people screamed. He opened his wings and allowed the wind to force him back up. The momentum carried him out of the range of the streetlights where the dark embraced him once again. His ascent slowed and he caught hold of the balcony rail on the top floor of the cathedral. The window had been bricked over and he flung himself from balcony to balcony along the side of the building just twelve feet down from the roof. The last of the balconies creaked under his massive weight and one of the brackets came dislodged from the brick. He let go and dropped the five stories into the dark.

* * *

James had been a teacher at one time. He had made the mistake of falling in love with a student. It was just a mistake. He never touched her. He loved her from afar and wrote poems to her. Her name was Doreen and she was nine at the time. She showed the notes to her mother and James was fired. "Bitch," James would say as he replayed the event in his mind, which only happened when he was drunk, which was every night. Lying in the alley with a bottle, he would replay the entire conversation in his brain over and over, only in his mind he would say all he wanted to say. In his mind he would explain himself properly. In his mind he would still think about Doreen and how pretty she was. She would be of age now. He wondered if she was still pretty. He wondered if he could go and find her. He wondered if God was still mad at him.

In that moment of that thought he became surprisingly lucid. In that moment of that noise, he thought maybe someone had pushed their refrigerator off a balcony and it had landed in the dumpster. He immediately corrected this idea and decided it was not a refrigerator but a Ford F550. Someone had managed to get a Ford F550 up on the roof of the building and had accidentally driven it off the edge. He covered his face with his hands, thinking maybe the shattering glass would cut his eyes. Surely there would be a fireball next. The gas tank would rupture and the vehicle and the cooking grease they illegally dumped in the dumpster would erupt and the entire alley would be in flames. James started to crawl away toward the edge of the alley. He felt something grab his ankle and pull him back. His fingers left marks on the filthy concrete. He felt himself lifted, and then he felt himself slammed against the brick wall higher up than anyone could reach. He looked from the edge of the alley to the face of what was holding him in place, and he knew he was dead.

He knew his body was lying somewhere under the wreck of the dumpster and that this was the devil. This was the face of Satan and it had come to take him to hell. James started to cry. "I didn't mean it," he said. "I didn't mean to hurt anyone. I don't want to go to Hell."

The black thing shook him and he screamed louder. The thing shook him several times until James got the idea that the louder he screamed, the more the thing shook him. James shut his mouth. The thing looked at him. It had a hundred teeth, easily a hundred on the top and the bottom and they fit together like the teeth of a hunting trap. It leaned in close. James felt its sandpaper skin brush his cheek. "You don't know what hell is," it whispered.

Then in one motion it threw James against the dumpster. Hard. He felt his teeth rattle; a few of them even came loose. His whole body shook with impact and he thought surely he had left as big a dent as the creature did when it landed. The thing was walking toward the edge of the alley. It didn't look back but James heard it say, "For the record? Yeah, He's still pissed at you."

Before the thing got to the street opening of the alley it ran toward the hard brick wall and scrambled up the side of the wall like a lizard.

***

Francis was feeling good about himself. He had a nice little buzz, courtesy of the packages he had stashed in his coat. He had been told to stay straight when he was at "work" but this was just a little buzz. Just a little buzz to get him through. He wasn't an addict or anything. Not like the people he was selling to. The ones who were really wasted, those are the ones to whom he would sell the bags that were just a little light. They wouldn't know. Some of them would probably even be dead later on. What would they do? Complain?

He was also happy because he had finally found a handle that seemed to stick. No matter what he called himself everyone still called him Francis. Last week he had corrected a junkie who had called him Francis. He had been with Thump. The customer had called Thump "Thump," but he had called Francis by his given name. Francis had thrown him on the ground and had kicked his face until he called him "Thrash." He didn't know where the name came from it just sort of popped into his head. He kicked the junkie until the junkie said, "Thrash" through his broken teeth. Francis had used the man's T-shirt to wipe the blood off the toe of his boot.

Now he was Thrash. Now he sat in his car parked along the street. Now he had a good little buzz and some respect and a pocket full of crank to sell to anyone who came up to the car.

Thrash knew he had a score when he saw the girl. She was pretty. She was young. Young and pretty. Thrash liked that. Easy to get them started. Probably raided Mommy's purse.

Thrash caught her eyes in his rear view mirror and smiled. He leaned out the window and said, "Hey, girly-girl. You want to take a little trip?"

CHAPTER FOURTEEN

Padi had planned her walk. First she would tell her mother she missed the bus. Then she would walk ten blocks to the hospital. She'd gone directly to the hospital after working at the church. She acted bored and slightly obnoxious and then told her mother she was going to the Terminal for supper. Her mother told her to take the bus and she promised to do that. She told herself that she did not promise to take the bus back to the hospital. It was a semantic point, but her mother seldom appreciated Padi's grasp of semantics.

She knew every store along the way. She could stop at the used music store, the used book store, and maybe the used clothing place although they had good sense to write "VINTAGE" on the sign and not "USED." She thought Vintage Vinyl might be a better name for the used music shop, and made a mental note to tell Jake the next time she saw him behind the counter. She would completely forget the idea before she ever made it to the hospital. She would forget just about everything about the walk.

Short-term memory loss is often a side effect of having the shit scared out of you.

She really liked Fr. Dark. He seemed to be a nice guy with a good sense of humor, and didn't at all seem like the kind of guy who would rat her out. That might be an act, of course—one of those ways they lull you into a false sense of security and then plaster your name on the prayer list under the heading "unspoken concerns," which most people automatically associate with either drugs or adultery. Fr. Dark didn't seem the type. She really wanted to be out tonight, despite the cold. She really wanted to see if the giant-flying-gorilla-monster would make a second appearance...because that would just be very cool.

There was a pair of black lace gloves in the vintage clothing place. She had visited them several times. Lace gloves with a flowery print that looked both delicate and incredibly slutty at the same time. Padi thought about the way old people talk about the good old days. "Yeah," she thought, "because with little clothing items like this everybody must have been 'doing it' all the time."

The gloves were $20. She tried them on again and looked at her hands in them. She wondered if the dark maroon nail polish would work with these. The church had not promised her any money for work she was doing, and her birthday was not until next year. She thought about putting the gloves on her Christmas list, but her mother would come into shop and take a look at the serious amount of eyeliner the clerk was wearing...think

Johnny Depp in the *Pirates* movies...and then walk out again.

Grandma's birthday money, maybe? Maybe if the church job went well she could pick up some freelance work? Fr. Dark seemed like a good guy he'd write her a reference letter, wouldn't he? Surely, Rev. Haberkorn would. She was thinking these thoughts and imagining the lace gloves on her hand while she typed. That would be her signature. People would remember that. They would shake her hand and notice the gloves but not say anything. Then later they'd get a little brave and ask how she did this kind of work with delicate gloves. She'd said, "It's delicate work." Okay, something better than that, but the gloves would be like a calling card. Someone would complain, "We need all new computers at the office and I don't know who to hire." Someone who was standing nearby would say, "We hired this girl. She was excellent. She wore these delicate lace gloves the whole time she worked. She owned her own business...it was..." Well, she'd have to think of a name for her company too, along with the snappy retort. Although "It's Delicate Work" would look really nice in a lace script beneath her name on a business card.

It was this she was thinking about, and not the number of blocks she had walked, when she finally looked. She had overshot her street by one—she turned around to walk back.

It should have been a nice car—it was a nice car but the idiot behind the wheel had let it go. He parked the car on the side of the street with the engine running and reved to get her attention. When she looked at him he was practically hanging out of the window. He called to her. "Hey girly-girl. You want to take a little trip?"

Her mother had taught her how to walk in the city. Don't make eye contact with anyone who looks scary, and don't *ever* stop walking. Just keep moving, even if someone comes up and asks you a question. Even if you give in and try to help someone out, don't ever stop moving and check your purse for your wallet. Keep a few singles in your coat pocket. Hand one of those to a homeless person, but don't ever stop. They can grab your purse and run—or worse, they can grab you.

When the man in the car asked if she wanted to take a little trip she didn't think he was offering her a ride. She knew what he was selling.

She had seen him before. This street was his sale aisle. He cruised up and down all night and called out to people. Sometimes they went to the window, sometimes they did not. She wondered what would happen if he got out of his car and followed her. She wondered what would happen if he got out of the car. She looked around to see which street she was on. Dontay lived around here, didn't he? Could she find his apartment building? He'd let her in if she needed it. The man in the rusting Corvette pulled ahead and then over to the curb. "Just one little trip. Go far and away from here. Tell you what, girlie-girl. First one is on me. First trip is a present from your old uncle Thrash."

Thrash.

Did he just call himself Thrash? How long had he been working on that one? She pictured him sitting in his apartment with a sheet of paper writing different nicknames down, like a school girl will write a boy's name down over and over. For some reason, this idiot thought Thrash would have a nice chilling effect on the general population. She could see her corner ahead. Left turn, and he would be behind her. "Come on, girlie-girl, let Thrash take you somewhere special."

Rule One: Don't make eye contact.

Rule Two: Don't stop moving...

Then there was Rule Three. Don't shout back at the idiots who yell things at you from cars. Then she broke them...all of them. One, Two, and Three....

"I'm sorry," she said, turning and stopping. "Did you say Trash?"

She saw his face darken. She turned and picked up speed toward the corner, cursing herself (with her mother's voice in her head), "Stupid, stupid, stupid, stupid, stupid." She pulled the hood of her sweatshirt over her head and promised to keep walking and not look back. Not looking back, she heard him stop the car and the door opened. "What'd you call me?" he said loudly.

She did not scream. This is something she would repeat to herself later on. She did not scream.

Thrash did.

His was not the first scream, though. The first scream belonged to a woman who had been coming out of a Chinese restaurant. She dropped her brown bag of food. Not so much dropping it, as launching it into the air where it hit the sidewalk and spilled lo mein on the dark pavement.

Padi turned and saw that something was standing on the top of Thrash's car. Something very big. Something that looked so big it was out of place. Nobody is that big. Not wrestlers on TV with their over-the-top steroid-enhanced muscles. Not the statue of Rocky Balboa in the park that once had been on the steps at the art museum. No, the thing on top of Thrash's car was much bigger. It was looking down at Thrash, and Thrash was looking smaller and smaller. Thrash had not yet fully emerged from the car, and he threw himself back behind the driver's seat and attempted to drive away. Padi was pretty sure he was crying.

The very large, very dark thing jumped down off the roof of the car and seemed, for a moment, to duck behind it. Thrash put the car in gear and the tires spun, but the car did not move. Instead the opposite side lifted up and the car came to rest on its side with the roof facing Padi. Now she was sure Thrash was crying.

In one motion, the very large, very dark thing took on a new descriptive word in Padi's mind.

Wings.

The very large, very dark thing had wings. It was on top of the car's side. Its wings were spread and the giant hand pushed through the glass passenger side window. It seemed to fish around for a moment, and then clutched onto something. As it turned out, the something was Thrash's hair. It was pulling the man completely out of the car through the passenger side window. More people screamed. Thrash would have, had he not had a hand over his mouth. His eyes, however screamed for him.

The very large, very dark thing with wings brought Thrash's face close to its own. First it brushed the long black Mohawk bangs from its face and then it smiled. Padi knew that there was nothing on earth that had that many teeth...at least nothing that could smile. It looked at Thrash and, like a mother straightening a child's hair on Sunday morning, brushed Thrash's greasy locks from his face. Then it spoke. Padi had never heard a voice like that before. It looked deep into Thrash's face and said, "Hello, Francis."

When she was a little girl, Padi's mother become very upset because Padi had a tendency to throw her dolls across the room. She wasn't trying to be mean to her dolls. It was just that when she was done playing with them she would simply toss them away. Her mother said she should keep her dolls in the toy crib that Santa has brought. But Padi still casually tossed them toward whatever toy-box or couch or chair was nearby. The very large, very dark thing with the wings and way too many teeth tossed Thrash (apparently his given name was Francis) across the sidewalk where he hit the brick wall with a sickening crack of bones. Before he could scream again, the creature was on him, hoisting him up and holding him against the wall. The two of them were only about six feet away from Padi, who had been so scared she had simply forgotten to move away.

The thing spoke to Thrash again. "Francis. What did you learn in school about drugs? Hmmmmm?"

Thrash/Francis began to shake as if he were having a seizure. The giant creature held Francis against the wall with its free hand and pulled the other from Francis/Thrash's mouth. "Oh, I'm sorry. Was it hard to breathe? Is that better?"

Francis/Thrash managed to get out a "na na na na na na na na na" sound. The creature smiled again, that awful smile, and said, "'Hey hey hey, gooooodbye,' I know that song."

At that moment it turned toward Padi and it spoke directly to her. "Go home."

Padi started to run. She ran down Fourth Street as fast as she could, her hood blowing off and tears falling from her eyes. Dozens of people were running in the opposite direction to see what was going on. Padi had no idea how she avoided colliding with any of them. She was three blocks away when she stopped running, her lungs aching for air. The November night was icy in her chest. She fell her to her knees and vomited twice into the sewer. She was still two blocks from the hospital.

She would forget everything about the walk: the vintage clothing store, the idea for a business card with black lace gloves. She would forget everything that happened right up until Thrash called her girlie-girlkid. What she would not forget...

what she would not be able to explain away out of her head...

was not the fact that the big dark scary thing with wings and too many teeth existed at all....

she had seen it...
she had heard it....
but something else.

Something she could not put her finger on until later and even then it was too much to tell anyone else. It was in the thing's eyes. It had looked directly at her. The big dark scary thing with the wings and too many teeth...had recognized her.

CHAPTER FIFTEEN

Andrew saw Glassman leaning against the wall.
He had one foot up against the wall. This meant he
was well stocked and ready to sell. If he had both
feet on the pavement that meant that he thought
that maybe he was being watched or his supply
hadn't arrived yet, so don't come up to him yet.
Andrew needed a hit bad. It had been a long week
by Tuesday, and he needed just a little to get him
through. He needed just one quick hit tonight and
then he would save the rest to get him the rest of
the way through to the weekend. Glassman saw
Andrew and smiled. He motioned with his chin and
stepped into the alley. Andrew waited a minute and
then crossed the street to follow him into the dark.
The alley stank of urine and rotting trash, but he
would only be there a minute. Andrew saw
Glassman reach into his pocket and pull the little
bag out and wave it at him. Andrew felt the inside
of his nose itch. He managed to keep himself from
rubbing it; that's what junkies did and Andrew
wasn't a junkie. Andrew reached into his pocket for
the money. When he looked up, he saw two gray

hands reach out of the darkness and grab Glassman from behind. Andrew saw the look of shock on Glassman's face, and then in an instant he was gone. Andrew stood there still holding the money in his hand. He looked at the spot where the Glassman had been standing and wasn't anymore. Looking—no, not just looking—peering into the darkness, squinting into the shadow Andrew saw something move. It was something very, very big. Andrew heard a voice that did not belong to Glassman. The voice, very quietly, said, "Go."

Six blocks later Andrew was still running and wondering what it was.

* * *

Susan had grown up with the name. Susan Johnson. Could you get anymore white bread America than Susan Johnson? Now she went by Sequin. She had taken it when she started dancing. She kept it when she went to work for Naws. She never told Naws her real name and he had never asked. She was used to it. He had taken her in. He had fed her. He had given her what she needed. He still did. He still provided. Naws didn't hit her near as much as he used to. He only hit her when he was angry or when business was slow or if he owed money to Cantrell. He would slap her with the back of his hand over and over. Almost never with his fists anymore. Fists damaged the merchandise. Slapping was about being put in your place, which is what he usually meant to do. She didn't know which it was tonight. She could see how angry he was from down the street. He was pacing and talking to himself. Not a good sign. Sometimes he would only hit her until she cried. Then he felt more like a man and he could put his arm around her and comfort her and explain how she had brought it on herself. She would nod her head and apologize and he would leave her alone again. Usually. If she cried too early he would just keep hitting. She had learned to gauge his moods pretty well.

She had money for him. Sometimes if she had extra she would hide some of it from him. Sometimes she would hide a little of the extra in an obvious place and then stash the majority somewhere else. He would ask her for the money and she would give it to him. He would ask for the extra and she would say there wasn't any extra. Then he would slap her and open her shirt and find what she had wanted him to find. He would slap her again and that would be the end of it. She had learned her lesson as far as he was concerned. Tonight he already looked upset. Something was very wrong. Tonight she would just give him everything right up front.

He was pacing back and forth behind the Italian restaurant, their usual meeting spot. There was a house, abandoned, next door that he liked to take her in sometimes when he was in the mood to be nice to her. She walked over to him smiling and reached into her purse. He slapped her hard before she said a word. "Hey, Bitch." He said it like a greeting.

She had also learned that if she rolled her head sometimes the slapping didn't hurt her as bad.

"You got paper for me, Bitch?"

She handed him a roll of bills. She had already sorted them in order of denomination. All the presidents were facing the same way. Just the way he liked. "What do you hear about Francis?"

She hadn't heard anything about Francis. "I don't know what you mean."

"Somebody messed up Francis," Naws said. "You supposed to keep you ears open and let me know what's going on."

"I haven't heard anything," she said.

"That's 'cause you stupid," Naws told her as he counted the money. "Where's the rest of it?"

"That's it," she told him, scared that he was getting really angry again. She wished she had held some back so she could give it to him now.

"That's never it," Naws said. "You think you can hide more from me but you know you can't. You stupid."

"That's all there is," she said again.

"First you don't pay attention to the street like I tell you, and then you try to steal from me. Haven't I been good to you?"

"Yes, Naws."

"Don't I take care of you?"

"Yes, Naws."

He drew back his hand, and she braced herself for the back of his hand. It didn't come. She opened her eyes to see Naws looking straight up into the eyes of something...something...she had no words for it. It looked like the gargoyles on top of the church but this one was bigger. This one moved. This one held Naws' hand above his own head so that his feet didn't touch the ground.

With one giant gray hand wrapped around Naws' wrist the thing reached over with its other hand and began to play with Naws' fingers. Naws was too scared to even move. His mouth was open but no sound was coming out. Susan started stepping backward very slowly. The thing looked over at her. "Don't move." She froze where she was.

The thing wiggled Naws' pinky finger with fingers that were three times the size of Naws'. It said, "Do I like to hit women?" Then it pushed Naws' finger backward in one swift motion. Susan heard the bone snap loudly. "Yes, Naws," the thing said.

The pain seemed to wake Naws up from his shock. He screamed and tried to get away. The thing said, "Does slapping women make me feel like I'm a big man who deserves respect?" The next finger snapped. Naws screamed. "Yes, Naws," the thing said.

Susan could see how the last two fingers on Naws' hand seemed to flap back and forth like they were no longer connected to anything on the inside.

"Pleeeeeeeeeease," Naws managed to say.

The thing grabbed Naw's middle finger. "Do I like to sell drugs and take money and ruin people's lives?" SNAP. "Yes, Naws."

The thing was sounding angry now. Susan thought she was more afraid of the calmness with which the giant thing had broken the first two fingers, then this one. Still she hadn't moved. The thing grabbed Naws' index finger. "Am I going to stop hitting women and stop selling drugs to children and STOP RUINING PEOPLE'S LIVES??" The thing waited. Naws, who was weeping by this time, took the hint and said, "Yes. Yesssss."

"Good answer," the thing said and then snapped the index finger too. Susan thought she heard the bones in Naw's wrist break too. The thing lifted Naws higher until they were face to face. "Whoever you report to, whoever is in charge, tell them this is my city and they will have to leave. What's the message?"

Naws, who Susan knew was a moron but was not stupid, said, "This is your city and they have to leave."

The thing set him down and let go of his wrist. Naws doubled over and fell to his knees, clutching his now worthless hand. He vomited on himself and fell over.

The thing stepped over Naws' motionless body and picked up the wad of cash on the ground. It walked toward Susan, who had not moved from the spot where it had told her to freeze. It carefully removed her sequin purse from her shoulder, opened the tiny clasp with its oversized gray finger, shoved the cash inside. Carefully, almost daintily, he snapped the purse closed and hung it back over Susan's shoulder.

Without another word it turned and walked casually around the side of the building and toward *the open street. Susan heard a scream. She heard brakes screeching. She heard the sound of bumpers colliding with fenders. Susan decided that maybe it was time to go home. She looked at Naws lying there on the pavement and wondered if her friend Mora could put her up for the night.*

* * *

Thump did not like this. He liked order. He liked pattern. He liked being in charge of people so afraid of him that they didn't dare deviate from the way he said things should be done.

His cell phone had not rung all night. None of his distributors had checked in. Not one of them. Six of them. Well, five and Francis who was now calling himself Thrash. Stupid name, thought Thump. All them couldn't have gotten busted on the same night, could they? Surely not all of them. Thump heard screams from the city below. From his place on the roof of the parking garage he could see so much. It was his kingdom. King Thump. It would be his kingdom someday. Cantrell would be gone. The trash would be moving out and the nice clean happy people would move in. The tourists would stay up where they were supposed to be. This part of the city would be renovated for the upwardly mobile. And the poor trash, well ,Thump really didn't care where they went. The nice clean happy people needed their recreational items as well. Thump knew this for a fact. Cantrell couldn't

*see past his own ugly face. Thump knew himself.
Thump was a man of vision.*

*Now he was looking down into the street. Even
from eight floors up he could recognize Eddie.
Eddie was his oldest distributor. Eddie always
played straight with him. Eddie took his bonuses
and smiled. Thump trusted Eddie in spite of the
silky shirts he liked to wear. Thump figured what
Eddie did on his own time was his own business
and he opened up a new clientele that Thump did
not like to deal with.*

*Something was dragging Eddie down the street.
Something very large. Something larger than himself. Something that was wearing what looked like
a cape.*

*Thump knew his business. Thump did not get
upset about losing a few employees. He opened his
cell phone and called Cantrell. The phone rang
once. "It's me," Thump said. "We have a problem."*

CHAPTER SIXTEEN

A STAR OVER THE I (EYE)
A blog about nothing, written for no one in particular,
by someone who pretty much stopped giving a rat's
ass about things a long time ago.

ENTRY #: Who the hell cares
HOLYCRAPHOLYCRAPHOLYCRAPHOLYCRAPHOLY-
CRAPHOLYCRAPHOLYCRAPHOLYCRAPHOLY-
CRAPHOLYCRAPHOLYCRAPHOLYCRAPHOLY-
CRAPHOLYCRAPHOLYCRAPHOLYCRAPHOLY-
CRAPHOLYCRAPHOLYCRAPHOLYCRAPHOLYCRAP
HOLYCRAPHOLYCRAPHOLYCRAPHOLYCRAPHOLY-
CRAPHOLYCRAPHOLYCRAPHOLYCRAPHOLY-
CRAPHOLYCRAPHOLYCRAPHOLYCRAPHOLY-
CRAPHOLYCRAPHOLYCRAPHOLYCRAPHOLY-
CRAPHOLYCRAPHOLYCRAPHOLYCRAPHOLYCRAP
HOLYCRAPHOLYCRAPHOLYCRAPHOLYCRAPHOLY-
CRAPHOLYCRAPHOLYCRAPHOLYCRAPHOLY-
CRAPHOLYCRAPHOLYCRAPHOLYCRAPHOLY-
CRAPHOLYCRAPHOLYCRAPHOLYCRAPHOLY-

CRAPHOLYCRAPHOLYCRAPHOLYCRAPHOLYCRAP
HOLYCRAPHOLYCRAPHOLYCRAPHOLYCRAPHOLY-
CRAPHOLYCRAPHOLYCRAPHOLYCRAPHOLY-
CRAPHOLYCRAPHOLYCRAPHOLYCRAPHOLY-
CRAPHOLYCRAPHOLYCRAPHOLYCRAPHOLY-
CRAPHOLYCRAPHOLYCRAPHOLYCRAPHOLYCRAP
HOLYCRAPHOLYCRAPHOLYCRAPHOLYCRAPHOLY-
CRAPHOLYCRAPHOLYCRAPHOLYCRAPHOLY-
CRAPHOLYCRAPHOLYCRAPHOLYCRAPHOLY-
CRAPHOLYCRAPHOLYCRAPHOLYCRAPHOLY-
CRAPHOLYCRAPHOLYCRAPHOLYCRAPHOLYCRAP
HOLYCRAPHOLYCRAPHOLYCRAPHOLYCRAPHOLY-
CRAPHOLYCRAPHOLYCRAPHOLYCRAPHOLY-
CRAPHOLYCRAPHOLYCRAPHOLYCRAPHOLY-
CRAPHOLYCRAPHOLYCRAPHOLYCRAPHOLY-
CRAPHOLYCRAPHOLYCRAPHOLYCRAPHOLYCRAP
HOLYCRAPHOLYCRAPHOLYCRAPHOLYCRAPHOLY-
CRAPHOLYCRAPHOLYCRAPHOLYCRAPHOLY-
CRAPHOLYCRAPHOLYCRAPHOLYCRAPHOLY-
CRAPHOLYCRAPHOLYCRAPHOLYCRAPHOLY-
CRAPHOLYCRAPHOLYCRAPHOLYCRAPHOLYCRAP
HOLYCRAPHOLYCRAPHOLYCRAPHOLYCRAPHOLY-
CRAPHOLYCRAPHOLYCRAPHOLYCRAPHOLY-
CRAPHOLYCRAPHOLYCRAPHOLYCRAPHOLY-
CRAPHOLYCRAPHOLYCRAPHOLYCRAPHOLY-
CRAPHOLYCRAPHOLYCRAPHOLYCRAPHOLY-
CRAPHOLYCRAPHOLYCRAPHOLYCRAPHOLY-
CRAPHOLYCRAPHOLYCRAPHOLYCRAPHOLY-
CRAPHOLYCRAPHOLYCRAPHOLYCRAPHOLYCRAP
HOLYCRAPHOLYCRAPHOLYCRAPHOLYCRAPHOLY-
CRAPHOLYCRAPHOLYCRAPHOLYCRAPHOLY-

CRAPHOLYCRAPHOLYCRAPHOLYCRAPHOLY-
CRAPHOLYCRAPHOLYCRAPHOLYCRAPHOLY-
CRAPHOLYCRAPHOLYCRAPHOLYCRAPHOLYCRAP
HOLYCRAPHOLYCRAPHOLYCRAPHOLYCRAPHOLY-
CRAPHOLYCRAPHOLYCRAPHOLYCRAPHOLY-
CRAPHOLYCRAPHOLYCRAPHOLYCRAPHOLY-
CRAPHOLYCRAPHOLYCRAPHOLYCRAPHOLY-
CRAPHOLYCRAPHOLYCRAPHOLYCRAPHOLYCRAP

HOLY CRAP HOLY CRAP HOLY CRAP ...AND IF I DID-
N'T SAY ENOUGH...HO-LEEE-CRAP!!!!!!

CHAPTER SEVENTEEN

I have a theory...

Let's say you assign headaches a numeric value from one to ten, based on intensity. That's the number of extra scoops of coffee grounds you add to your coffeemaker to get rid of the headache. I was working on a number five headache. I prepared a pot of coffee and then added five extra scoops. Okay, it's not a scientific theory but it's mine. Einstein wasn't even close, by the way, so give me a break.

I had discovered that the fruity-doughy thingies warm up just fine in the microwave, but the "ding" of the timer when you have a number five is like a railroad spike being driven through your temple. I would imagine that number eight would kill you. Number ten? You probably shouldn't be out of bed with a number ten. I still had not yet gone to the grocery store, so there was not one aspirin in the whole apartment. I had a staff meeting in a little more than an hour in which I was going to be meeting most of the staff and they were going to be meeting the new associate and I looked and felt like I had rung the Liberty Bell with my forehead. I eased myself into the couch with my coffee and red fruity-doughy thingy and turned on the TV.

I scanned the local television channels hoping for a Good-Morning-Philadelphia type program. My adopted city did not disappoint. A perky young woman with unnaturally blonde hair was trying to look serious in her Neiman-Marcus blouse. *"...conflicting reports about just what did attack the citizens of Philadelphia's lower East Side last night."*

Attack? Who attacked?

"...reports of a flying gorilla have come from witnesses who were on the scene."

A flying gorilla?

"...description included, giant bat, demon, and eight-foot zombie with wings."

Zombie. I liked that.

"...four men were taken to the hospital last night after witnesses say they were randomly pulled out of a crowd and beaten...."

Randomly? Wasn't random at all. And why only four? Who decided they shouldn't go to the emergency room?

The screen was suddenly filled with eyewitness reports. First there was a young man in his twenties. He looked a little bleary-eyed in the camera lights. The background behind him was still night. This boy wasn't going to have a whole lot of credibility.

*"Man, it was like...you know...and then...
whoosh...it looked like one of those orcs from the*
Lord of The Rings *movie."*

Great, now I was an orc. I needed to go and rent
this movie. The screen switched to an older man in
a tie.

*"...shouldn't allow these kids out here at night.
The whole lot of 'em are all hopped up on dope."*

Dope?

A young woman appeared and said, *"It scared
the (bleep) out of me. The thing turned a car over,
you know? How does one guy turn a car over?"*

Finally, my TV held the familiar face of Miss
Roberta. Dontay's grandmother. The scene behind
her was light so I was guessing that she had been
filmed earlier this morning. She shared the screen
with on-the-street-reporter Ken Duffy, who for
some reason was wearing his raincoat, probably
left over from the last big tornado remote. The
word at the top right-hand side of the screen said
"Live."

"Here we go," I thought.

"Megan," said Ken on-the-street, "I'm here live
getting reactions to the attacks from citizens of
Philadelphia." He pointed the microphone at
Roberta, who gave him the same "Shut up, sonny"
look she had given me. This is what she said:

*"I don't for a minute believe that innocent peo-
ple were attacked. If someone wants to come
downtown and beat the living crap out of drug
dealers, then I say more power to them."* She
looked at the reporter, who seemed stunned.

My guess was that she had promised to be the scared old lady on camera and then pulled a switch on him. "You go, Roberta."

I stood up, too quickly apparently, and lost my balance and had to sit back down. I stood up slowly and made my way to the bathroom. I could probably get a shower and go visit Dwight before my staff meeting. I wondered if some of my co-workers (the ones with white fluffy wings) had the same hangover problem. I would have to ask, but it's not like we have a convention or anything.

I stood there in the shower and let the hot water spray me in the forehead until it felt like the pain had washed down the drain. Good water pressure for an old building. I was half dressed and walked out into the living room to see an extremely stoic-looking redhead in a nice suit on the screen. The words under her image read Press Conference, Detective Maggie Grafton. I turned it up. You could tell she had just about had it with the reporters. There was just a hint of an Irish accent that I was guessing only came out when she was pissed.

"...do *not* encourage the citizens of Philadelphia to take the law into their own hands. The men who were attacked do have arrest records but that does not account for the brutality with which they were attacked. As of yet, we have no photographs or accurate images of the attacker. We are asking anyone with information, or who might have taken a picture with their phone, to come forward."

A reporter off-camera asked something unintelligible and Detective Grafton looked as though she was doing all she could not to pull out her revolver and shoot him.

"At this time," she said, as if she were repeating it for a four-year-old, "Because of the associations and history of those who were harmed, we are looking at this from the point of view of it being gang-related. If we gain any evidence to the contrary, we will follow that evidence, but right now we are assuming the individual or individuals who perpetrated these crimes did so as an act of gang violence."

Someone else stared to speak, but the detective said, "That's all." It was a firm dismissal and she turned her back and disappeared back under a piece of yellow crime scene tape.

In my black shirt and collar (and another pair of chucks), I grabbed my coat and headed down the stairs. There is an elevator, which I may use to come back up but it was slow and I could probably run down the stairs before the elevator got to my floor.

In the lobby I met Rev. Haberkorn. He said, "Good morning, Michael. I wanted to talk with you for a few moments before the staff meeting. Do you have a minute?" He put his hand on my shoulder and I could feel the wisdom inside this man. I half wanted to bow and call him Obi-wan.

"I was just on my way to get a cup of coffee. Would you like to walk with me?"

He smiled and said, "I heard you are quite the coffee hound."

I looked back over my shoulder at Alice who was

trying to look like she wasn't looking at me. Rev. Haberkorn and I started out the door. When we were on the street, he put his hands in his pockets and said, "I need to tell you this." We waited for a semi to pass by. "There are people in the church who believe that the priest is every bit a part of the building as the stained glass windows and the pews." I nodded. I had known a few people like that.

"There are other people who believe that knowledge equals power and will take in as much as they can and give out as little as possible."

"What are you saying?" I asked as we reached the door to Java Joe's.

"I'm saying learn how to use the back door."

I wondered for a moment why he was mentioning this and then he said quietly, "Alice keeps track of just about everybody and everything. She's good at her job, but she keeps a list. Do you know what I mean?"

I nodded. The light blinked as we went through the door. Dwight looked up and I signed, "Two coffees." I said it out loud at the same time. "And a muffin." I looked at Rev. Haberkorn. "Something for you?"

He looked puzzled for a second and then chuckled. "At least I know you'll stay awake in the staff meeting." He ordered a hot chocolate, and three minutes later we were back on the street. As we crossed the street, I looked back into the coffee shop and there sitting at a table was Sequin. Her make-up was gone and I nearly didn't recognize her. She looked up and managed a weak smile in my direction. I said to Haberkorn, "I forgot the cream. I'll catch up with you."

"We're in the conference room on the second floor," he said and finished crossing. I went back into the shop and walked over to Susan's table.

"Hey father," she said.

"May I sit?" I asked.

She shrugged. I sat. She looked out the window. "You're new," she said.

"Just started," I said. "I almost didn't recognize you."

"I don't know a lot of priests who drive around in the middle of the night," she said, referring to my arrival.

"I just got into town. Couldn't get into my apartment yet."

She seemed to understand this. She still had not looked at me. The silence got a little awkward. I said, "Look, I've got a meeting in a few minutes. I sat down because you looked like you needed someone to talk to. If you want to talk, I can be back in a hour so."

She said, "Yeah, as long as I eat I can have a seat." She looked over at Dwight, who was busy. I saw she had no food in front of her, so I handed her the muffin in a bag and said, "I'll be back and we'll talk."

I stood and caught Dwight's eye on the way out. He looked at me. He didn't need to sign. The look spoke for him. "Do you know what you are doing?"

"Truthfully? No," I smiled back and went out the door. One of these days I was actually going to eat one of those muffins.

My good friend and new role model, Miss Roberta, was sitting behind the desk when I came in. "Miss Roberta." I smiled. "I saw you on TV this morning." She grinned and patted her hair like she was primping for the camera. "What brings you here?"

She said, "I come in on Staff Meeting days to answer the phone while Alice takes notes during the meeting."

"You seem to do a lot here."

"My husband and I were very active. When he passed, my church family gathered around me and kept me going, so I do what I can."

There was a joy in her that just made me smile. I asked, "Will we be seeing Dontay after school today?"

"Oh yes," she said. "You might want to talk to him, Reverend." Then she lowered her voice and her chin and I bent over to listen to her whisper. "I think," she said, "that my grandson knows something about that thing that turned over the cars."

I wanted to tell her it was just one car, but what I said was, "He was out last night?"

"No," she said, "I mean from before. Yesterday I caught him doing his own laundry and I recognized the smell. He had wet himself. Then this morning before school he was reading the paper and then, bam, he was off like a shot. No breakfast, no 'good-bye, grandma,' no nothing."

"He was reading about the gangs?" I asked.

"Wasn't no gang," she corrected. "I heard tell it was one big scary man in some kind of costume."

I said, "How did one man turn over so many cars?" Yeah, I know what you're thinking, but I had to see if I could build it up a little.

She told me, "I don't know. But just by the way Dontay read that paper, I could tell what had scared him so bad the night before." She leaned back. I stood up. She said, "You're late."

I hustled for the elevator.

Saint Marjorie's had some good people on its staff. Rev. Haberkorn. The music director, whose name was John Buffet but who was no relation to Jimmy (I know because that's the first question I asked—apparently it's the first question *everybody* asks). And a woman named Anne, who wore her hair tight and curly, was the missions director. Anne's favorite phrase, I was soon to learn, was "What is the church going to do about...."

It didn't matter what you were talking about—she simply filled in the blank. "What's the church going to do about condoms in schools?"

"What's the church going to do about women in the workplace?"

"What's the church going to do about government spending?"

It was like a strange and bizarre Mad Lib. I wanted to come up with something like "cheese steaks" and see if I could get her to question the church's role in the great Gino's vs. Pat's debate. Sort of a "What Would Jesus Eat?" discussion.

Sitting at the end of the table directly opposite the music director (and when I say "directly opposite" I mean that in the truest sense of the word) was Miss Dorothy McConelly. Miss McConelly was a short woman, around sixty, and about the width of a drinking straw. She dressed like something a four-year-old had colored. Her dress was bright purple, her stockings bright yellow, her blouse was pink, and her black suit jacket was fairly normal except for a *huge* pin that looked like a handmade sculpture of our Lord and Savior. The artist (who I'm guessing was eight at best) depicted Christ as a rather plump individual. He held the bread and the cup in his hands—and one could easily imagine the bread as a cheese steak, but I don't believe that was the artist's intention. She came into the room giggling, she left the room giggling, and pretty much giggled at everything everyone said (except for our discussion about "what the church should do about this flying demon situation").

Dorothy also had a massive coffee mug. It said "Jesus Loves Me" in bright friendly letters over a rainbow. Right away I felt comfortable enough with her to ask if the coffee counted as proof of that statement. She giggled. She came in with an armload of books and papers and just seemed to spread out on her end of the table.

Mr. Buffet (I don't think I'll ever be able to call him John) sat at the other end in his tweed jacket with a small black notebook and a single pen, which he had laid side by side until the meeting started. Lucas Haberkorn, the quiet, sat at the head of the table with Alice sitting about six inches from his left (clearly placing herself above the rest of us). And then there was me. The new guy.

Let me tell you one story about Dorothy. I got this from Jack the property manager (who conveniently scheduled a delivery of toilet paper during the meeting and had to sign for the delivery). He said about four or five years ago that Dorothy and Rev. Haberkorn were walking down the hallway toward the famous back entrance. The bottom floor of the cathedral is a nursery school during the week. Dorothy acts as a sort of chaplain to the school but she doesn't run it. Dorothy and Rev. Haberkorn took one step out the back door and saw a man of less than desirable reputation talking to one of the little girls. She was all dressed in pink and pigtails, and he was right in the process of taking his wiener out to show it to her. He was trying to hold her with one hand and pull himself out with the other when the door opened and there was these two short people, one in a clergy collar, and one in day-glo orange.

The girl was crying. Mr. Oscar Mayer immediately let go and started to run. The little girl came screaming toward Dorothy and Haberkorn. Dorothy ran right past the little girl and went after the guy who was running across the rear parking lot with his hoo-ha flapping in the breeze. Haberkorn had the girl in his arms and was taking her back inside. Dorothy was still chasing the pedophile. Suddenly he turned and thought (maybe since he's all of six feet tall and, apparently, a guy) that he could take on a sixty-year-old skinny woman in heels.

Bad idea. According to Jack, she put one of those high heels in the center of his forehead and then pinned him to the blacktop with a move she learned in self-defense class. Now I also heard this story from Padi, my little computer hacker, who said that Dorothy used the high heel in another area that the pedophile, in a clear bit of bad strategy, had left exposed to the elements. Either way, he went down—and he went down hard.

The girl was fine. She was never harmed. Mr. Tallywacker was sentenced to six months (*six months?*) and was ordered to stay at least one hundred yards from the nursery school during business hours (which he apparently thought meant that he could sleep in the alley beside the school at night). The police department officially told Dorothy that a citizen taking the law into her own hands was not a good idea because the man could have been armed. UNofficially, she is quietly saluted by almost every cop on the block. The girl's parents did not insult Dorothy by offering a cash thank-you (honestly, what kind of price do you put on something like that?). They did, however, speak to Dwight across the street and fix it so that she would never ever have to pay for another cup of coffee for the rest of her life. I'm jealous. I'm in awe but I'm still jealous.

If you think God reserves a special place for waitresses in heaven, you should see the set-up for those who rescue children.

Most of the meeting was spent unofficially grilling the new associate. As far as they were concerned the diocese assigned me to them. I'm sure they all took a look at the bio that Gabriel had planted on the web site. (Even I was able to access it by watching Padi. I have to admit, I was pretty impressed with my history.) I was able to bluff my way through a few anecdotes about former co-workers and growing up in Cleveland.

When Anne began with, "What's the church going to do about the demon situation?" I knew I was in trouble.

No one at the table believed there was anything Biblical or demon-ish involved. And since there were no pictures they all assumed it was one guy or perhaps more than one guy in a costume who had a vendetta against the dealers in this area. Most of the table believed that that the police or the gangs would put a stop to it...eventually.

Yeah...yeah...I know what you're thinking. I was thinking the same thing.

* * *

Two and one-half hours later the meeting ended with all of us fully informed about each other's activities. My list was comparatively short given that I had only been at the church for a few days. I was, however, going to do a sermon at Children's Chapel on Sunday morning—some time after the seven o'clock mass (at which I was presiding) and before the nine o'clock mass (where I was assisting the Rev. Haberkorn).

I bolted out of the meeting to meet Susan across the street. Okay, I bolted out of the meeting to pee and *then* I bolted out of the building to see Susan. Happy now?

I got across the street to Java Joe's and she was gone.

* * *

Later that afternoon I sat in my own guest chair (again) as Padi sat in my office chair (again) tapping away at my keyboard.

"How do I know you aren't planning to launch nuclear weapons from my computer?" I asked her as I tossed an M&M in the air and caught it in my mouth.

"I'm not allowed on those sites anymore," she said. I honestly couldn't tell if she was kidding or not.

"I've got you set up with an account at a place called Ugly Mug Coffee," she said.

"I'm intrigued. What does that entail?"

"Well," she said, "as far as they're concerned, the church is actually doing the ordering so you won't pay any taxes and they'll give you a special business rate. All you have to do is drink lots of coffee."

"I think I can do that," I said. I fished a blue one out of the bowl and she said, "Gimme the blue."

I tossed it. She opened her mouth and it bounced off her lower lip and onto my desk. She picked it up and ate it.

"Try again," she said. I tossed her another one and she caught it, throwing her arms in the air in an "It's *good!*" motion.

I put the bowl on the desk and scooted the guest chair back about six feet. "Long shot," I said.

She picked up a red M&M and I said, "No. Gimme a yellow one."

She said, "They're more aerodynamic?"

"No, they just taste better."

She looked at me. "They all taste the same."

I said, "No they don't."

"You're thinking of Skittles."

I smiled and said, "I bet you I can tell the difference between colors solely by taste."

She said, "No way." I just smiled. She said, "No way," again.

At that point, Dontay came into the room. Padi said, "He says he can tell the different colors of M&M's by taste."

Dontay shook his head. "Can't be done. They're all the same."

I smiled at him too.

"I bet you can't," Padi said.

I said, "You pull out ten M&Ms. I'll tell you what color they are by taste, and if I miss just one, then you win."

"What do I win?"

"I'll buy you a one of those frappa-dappa latte coffee things from over at Java Joe's. But if I can…"

"Which isn't possible," she put in.

"Which is entirely possible." I continued, "You have to stay out of my chair."

She looked at Dontay. He smiled and said, "Do it."

"You sit over here," she said to Dontay.

He moved and she came around to my side of the desk. I took off my pastor's glasses and put my hand over my eyes. "No way," She said, "You'll cheat." She put her own hands over my eyes and told Dontay to pull out an M&M. I heard his fingers rummage in the bowl as if there might be a lone puce candy at the bottom. Finally I opened my mouth and felt one drop in.

I should point out here that I have met one human being who could actually tell yellow M&Ms from the other colors, but no one I've met can pick out all of them. And if you want to get all Christian on me, I suppose this was actually cheating because I was using my guardian powers to distinguish color—but I justify this by saying it was bonding me to the youth group, which would come in handy later. The first one was red.

I said, "Red" right away.

Padi took her hands off my eyes. "You cheated."

I said, "How did I cheat? You covered my eyes."

She looked at me and said, "Then it was luck."

"Nine more to go," I said. "If it was luck then I'll probably miss one." I didn't. She kept both hands firmly over my eyes and Dontay tossed M&Ms into my mouth.

They went in this order.

Red

Yellow

Green

Blue
Red
Blue
Orange

At this point I heard Padi say, "Not that one." I smiled. "What? Are you coaching him?"

"That one," she said, still with her hands over my eyes.

The next four went like this

Yellow
Yellow
Yellow
Yellow

After the fourth one I said, "You think you can fool me?"

Dontay said, "There's no way. He can see or you're giving him signals."

"I'm not," she said.

"I have very sensitive taste buds," I said. I stuck out my tongue showing them the remnants of the last four candies.

"Man, that's gross," Dontay said.

"One more. Double or nothing?"

"Just give him one more," Padi said. She had resigned herself to defeat. To be honest I thought about missing the last one on purpose, but I decided that I would buy her the coffee anyway, thereby upping my cool points and getting my chair back in the process.

The last one was blue. "Blue," I said.

And she stepped back and said, "There's no way."

"I told you," I said. "I have sensitive taste buds. All the men in my family could tell the difference." This of course was a lie. My father never had an M&M in his life. He had seen a preacher eat grasshoppers and honey and tried it himself. They weren't half bad. He also liked dried sugar dates, but they gave him the runs.

She leaned against the desk with her arms folded. "You must have some way of seeing."

"Actually," I said, "a guy I went to seminary with had a sister who worked for the Mars Company. She used to send him four-pound bags and he and I both got pretty good at telling the difference."

"But you got ten out of ten," she protested.

"I was better at it."

"I still don't believe it."

I reached into my back pocket to get my wallet. "Tell you what, I'll still buy you a cup of coffee, right now, and all you have to do is bring me one too."

She reached for my ten and I pulled it back. "*And*," I said, "you still have to keep your butt out of my chair."

She took the ten and went out the door. "Mocha!" I yelled after her. "Extra whipped cream!"

She was gone. I could hear the elevator doors open in the hallway. I looked at Dontay and he looked at me. He was smiling. Something I hadn't seen on him yet.

"How'd you do it?" he asked.

"Magic," I said, and waved my spirit fingers in the air like David Copperfield, or maybe it was Kristin Dunst. I didn't remember. (Gabriel took away my Blockbuster card.) "Sometimes the impossible is totally possible, no matter how much you want to believe otherwise. Sometimes things just are."

I looked at him and watched the smile fall away from his face.

"Your grandmother told me you kinda freaked out this morning. Is that true."

He was going to deny it. I could see it in his face. He put his hands in his lap and suddenly looked like he was two instead of a teenager.

"I saw somethin'," he said.

"What did you see?"

"You won't believe me."

"You'd be surprised what I believe," I whispered, and leaned in close to the front of my own desk.

He leaned in as well. He had been sitting on this without telling anybody and he was ready to bust. He said, "Do you believe in demons, Reverend?"

I said, "You mean like in the movies? Like possessed people?"

He shook his head. "Like big things that come outta hell."

"I've never seen one."

He said, "You know that thing they were writing about in the papers?"

"The gang thing?" I asked.

"Wasn't no gang," he said. "It was one big thing."

"What do you mean?" I asked. I wondered if he was going to own up to the crack. Had I scared him that much?

"Was one big scary motherfucker," he said. He didn't flinch at the curse and I did him the favor of not flinching as well. Plus, it was probably the most accurate way he knew to describe what had gotten to him.

"You saw it?" I asked. "Up close?"

His eyes started to well up and he was reliving the experience. I felt sorry for him and then decided it was probably better this way.

He looked past me to my office door, as if checking if Padi was coming back. "She'll be another ten minutes." I said.

He looked at the top of my desk. "It grabbed me," he said quietly. "It looked at my face and it scared me so bad I pissed myself."

"What was it?" I asked. "Some kind of mask?"

He shook his head. "It was real. I know it wasn't no mask. It was too big. Had teeth and bad breath and it burned my soul patch." He tapped his chin. "My grandma thinks I shaved it off but that thing burned it off with its finger."

I was silent for just a second and then I asked, "Why did it come and get you?"

He hesitated. Then he looked me right in the eye and said, "It was a dark angel. It told me to quit doing drugs and to clean up my act."

I waited to see if he would tell me more, but he

was waiting to see my reaction to his drug admission. Finally I said, "What kind of drugs were you doing?"

"Crack," he said. "I only did it one other time. I done some weed but I only did crack the one time other than two nights ago. I thought I had dreamed the whole thing but then I saw it the paper and I knew it was real. It was a real thing. It wasn't human."

I leaned back in my chair and he let one tear fall out of his eye. He wiped it away quickly. "You not gonna tell my grandma, are you?" he asked. "She said if I ever do drugs she'll kick me out of the house."

"Are you going to do them again?" I asked.

"Are you shitting me?" he said. "I'm more afraid of that demon thing than I am my grandma, and that's saying something."

I said, "First, I'm not going to tell your grandmother—but I want you to talk to somebody. I know a drug counselor (which wasn't true but I thought I could find one pretty easily). You talk to her, and if she gives me the okay then it stays between you and me. Deal?"

He nodded.

"As for the other thing...I'm not going to lie to you, Dontay. It's hard to believe. Will you at least give me that? That it's hard to believe? I'm not going to say I don't, because there are a lot of possibilities in this world, but you at least have to give me that it's hard."

He nodded again. I said, "We'll talk more about it tomorrow."

"Good," he said, "'cause I ain't going out at night again. Ever."

Padi came back with the coffees. "I got it," she said. "You and Dontay worked it out yesterday. You're conning me."

"Dontay, did you assist me in a con against Padi?"

He half-smiled and shook his head.

"Do it again," she said, handing me my cup. "I want to see you do it again, and this time I pick all the colors."

CHAPTER EIGHTEEN

Von Hayes was being cautious. He was just going to make his rounds, collect his fees, and go home. That was it. Nothing special. Nothing out of the ordinary. Not tonight. In fact he was going to do less than the ordinary. He wasn't going to get a hooker tonight. He wasn't going to even drink at the bar. He had beer at home. That's all he would need: beer and the Spice channel. Tomorrow he would pay Thump in the light of day and then he would go home again. He would wait for this to blow over. Whoever was beating the shit out of Cantrell's men hadn't been caught yet. The police would catch him...or them. Von Hayes knew that. They would catch these guys and put them away because even the bad guys had rights. Right?

This is what he told himself as he drove across Independence Avenue toward the south side. Von Hayes had a nice little apartment just outside of the historic district. It was small but nice. He had a neighbor, Mrs. Halverson, who thought he was a

*contractor and worked a lot at night. He had once
helped her with her groceries and she'd tipped him
a quarter. He'd stolen fifty dollars from a cup in her
cupboard while he helped her put the groceries
away. She'd asked him about it a few days later and
he told her a story about his own grandmother and
how she'd always forgotten when she spent money.
This was a lie, of course. Jason Von Hayes had
never known his grandparents...any of them. His
father and mother had been arrested for mail fraud
and had both gone to prison. He'd gone into the
foster system until he was eighteen, and then gone
to work for Thump. Nearly ten years of gainful
employment. He had a new car (well, used, but last
year's model) and a good apartment and nearly
$200,000.00 in the bank. No, he was not stupid.
He was going to sell this load and lay low until the
police did their job and got this nutcase off the
street.*

*He dialed his cell phone. "Dewboy!" he shouted,
all friendly-like as if he wasn't worried at all.
"Dewboy, it's Von Hayes. You up for a party
tonight? ...Dude, it's totally safe.... Hey, I'm out
here ain't I? ...Nah, nah, nah...coincidence,
buddy.... Thrash...had an accident.... It was an
accident, Dewboy. Man, do you know anybody
who can flip a car over by themselves? ...Nah...me
neither, so it had to be an accident. Thrash was
stoned and was seeing things and made up a story
to make up for the fact that he pissed himself when
he wrecked.... Yeah, I'm sure."*

The cell phone beeped in his ear.

"Dewboy, I got another call, you want the party planner or not? I only got a limited amount so if you don't want it now.... That's my Dewboy.... Usual spot? ...Later."

Von Hayes hit a button on the cell.

"Thump. Talk to me, what the hell is going on? ...I mean, I'm out here and I'm just about the only one you got left and I'm having a hard time moving my own stuff tonight. People are scared shitless."

Von Hayes made a left on 17th Street.

"I'm saying, you got to find out what's giving people the wiggles or you're gonna be out of customers."

Two large feet landed on the hood of his new car and stopped it on the spot. There was no screeching of tires, as there were no brakes applied. The engine simply broke through the bottom of the frame and embedded itself in pavement. The deep dent in the hood looked like someone had dropped a bus on it.

At the moment of impact, Von Hayes was thrown forward smashing his teeth into the steering wheel breaking the front four. He tried to swear but he had also bitten off the end of his own tongue. Still holding the phone with one hand, Von Hayes covered his mouth with the other. He looked out the window and saw the feet. They weren't human. Every justification, every theory, every rational formula that he had come up with for what had taken out Thrash, Glassman, and Francis blinked out of his memory and was replaced by one thought. "The

*devil got them." This thought was replaced by
"The devil is going to eat me."*

*Two very large, very dark, very scaly hands
broke through the left side of his windshield and
lifted the glass out in mostly one piece. He heard
the bits of glass hit his hood and his front seat. He
heard the bulk of the windshield hit the building to
his left. He heard the horns. He heard the screams.
He heard Thump on the other end of the phone
shouting something. And from the thing on the
hood, he thought he heard laughter.*

*The two hands now reached in and, with no
effort whatsoever, lifted him from the drivers seat.
The pain in his teeth and nose was nothing compared to the fear that swept over him in the next
second. He was lifted out of his new car (well, used,
but last year's model) and found himself face to
face with something he had no reference point to
define. Later in the hospital, when he was handcuffed to the bed rail (thank God), he would try
and think if he was nose to nose with the thing, but
couldn't say that because he couldn't remember a
nose. Not a human nose anyway. Maybe more like
a snout. But not a snout. Not really even a face.
Except for the eyes. Later, when he was in the hospital handcuffed to the bedrail and trying to give a
description to the cop artist, he thought about
those eyes again and started crying. He cried like a
baby and had to be sedated. He made a promise to
himself that he would never think about those eyes
again.*

That would be tomorrow. Right now he was

looking into those eyes and they were looking, quite literally, into him. He could feel them piercing the back of his skull right through his own eyes. That thing's eyes were not at all human. He swore he could smell those eyes and it was turning his stomach.

The thing gently pulled the cell phone out of his hand and brought it to its massive face. The face that was so big the cell couldn't reach both its mouth and its ear at the same time. The thing said into the cell, "He's busy. He'll call you back." Von Hayes thought he felt the voice down into his toes. It wasn't at all human either. He was only vaguely aware that his shirt was smoking. The thing held him aside and reached down into his passenger seat. It grabbed his leather bag, the bag with 50 grand of crank under its false bottom and held it over its shoulder. Von Hayes had a comic vision of the way he was being carried. The front of his shirt was smoking and he was being carried like he wasn't even in it. He was being carried like a pile of dirty laundry.

He bumped his head into several cars as he was carelessly dragged along for the ride as the giant thing jumped from car roof to car roof. Just before he felt himself leave the ground, he noticed the wings. The image of the street disappearing beneath him would have been much more traumatic if he hadn't seen the wings.

* * *

He felt himself dangling. He felt the cold air rush by him. It made his broken teeth hurt. He recognized the police station beneath him. He had been there before. The thing was now holding onto the front of the building by its toes. It held him with one hand twenty feet above the entrance. Von Hayes coughed and sprayed blood up and it fell back into his face. The thing draped the bag of crank over his neck. Then it brought him close to that face again and said, "You owe Mrs. Halverson fifty dollars."

Von Hayes managed to say, "Please don't drop me," just before it did.

CHAPTER NINETEEN

Thump resisted the urge to throw the phone against the brick wall. He'd lost too many that way. He decided it would be much more satisfying to crush it with his big hand but managed to keep from doing that as well. He had been working on his anger issues. He had joined a yoga class and was learning to control his rage. The only male in the class and easily twice the size of anyone else in the room, Thump had been learning to find his center and to breathe.

He took a deep breath through his nose and let it out through his mouth. He took another one, and then picked up a garbage can and flung it down the alley like a forest ranger skipping a stone across a pond. The clanging sound was incredibly satisfying. He felt much better.

He was running out of distributors quickly. It seemed as though Von Hayes would be on his disabled list for a while. (He had no idea.) He still had The Baker on the east side and Totem downtown.

Thump liked Totem. He was into all that mystical shit and how certain narcotics in the right combination could make you visit other dimensions. Totem was older than Thump, but had no thoughts of career advancement and he never worked stoned. As long as he could afford his rent, his food, and his own stash, he didn't care about much else. He never tried to cheat Thump out of more than the occasional ten percent, and that was built into the cost, so Thump let it go. Besides, Totem made him smile.

The Baker gave Thump the creeps. He always smelled like cinnamon and made comments to Thump about the women he had been with. How he liked to use meth to get them "all hot and ready" and then usually waited until they passed out before he took them to his bed. "Like doin' it with the dead," The Baker had said. Thump didn't like The Baker but he had an extensive client list in areas of the city that Thump didn't like to go. The Baker had cheated Thump one time and Thump had broken his pinky finger. The Baker never did it again. Thump did not ask what The Baker did with his money. The Baker just wanted to make Thump happy. Thump just wanted to make Cantrell happy. If Cantrell was happy then everybody was happy. They were all one big happy family in the City of Brotherly Love.

Thump had a dozen second-stringers that he did not trust and a few bangers that he trusted a little to handle some of the blood work but that was it. Most of his first-string team was gone.

Thump saw Dontay before Dontay saw him. "Don-*tay*!" Thump called. Dontay walked faster. Thump pinched the bridge of his nose and then started walk faster himself. People parted for him easily. Not just because of his size but because when he walked he could put on this face that said, "Get the fuck outta my way." People did. It was like a mental cow pusher. Even guys who were almost Thump's size cleared a path rather than piss off a tank.

"Don-*tay*," Thump called. Dontay did not look, but ducked into a coffee shop. Thump walked past the coffee shop at a steady pace and then stepped into the next available alley. It was only a few minutes later that Dontay came walking by, all calm and relaxed again.

Thump grabbed him and dragged him into the alley. "Dontay," Thump said, "you didn't hear me calling you?"

Dontay reached up and removed the earbuds from his ears and said, "What?" Dontay's ear buds weren't connected to anything. Someone had stolen his iPod on the subway last month. It had been his fourth, but he had only paid for one of them anyway so he had been keeping the buds in his pocket until he could steal another one, maybe even get his own back again. He'd put the earbuds in when he left the coffee shop, just for situations like this one.

"I got some sweet for you, man," Thump said.

"I got no bills." Dontay said.

"I tell you what," Thump said. "I'll give you two rocks and you can pay me for one later. The other one I'll give you for free just for information."

"What could I tell you that you don't already know?" Dontay said, smiling.

Thump smiled back. He liked it when people tried to blow smoke up his ass.

Thump pulled a small plastic bag out of his pocket and tried to shove it down Dontay's shirt. Dontay wriggled like it was going to burn him and the packet fell on the floor of the alley. Both of them looked at it, Dontay like he wasn't going to ever pick it up, and Thump like he couldn't believe Dontay wasn't picking it up. When did this kid grow a pair?

Thump let it lie on the cement and looked at Dontay. "I need to know why my guys are in the hospital. Can you help me with that information?"

Dontay said, "I don't know anything.'

Thump shook him and Dontay felt his teeth rattle. "Is it FBI? DEA? Some other gang trying to come in and mess with my men?"

Dontay said, "Wasn't no gang."

"What was it, then?"

Dontay said nothing and Thump shook him again violently. He repeated, "What was it, then?"

"Wasn't human," Dontay said. "Was big. Mean. But it wasn't human."

"We need to reduce your dosage, man. You seeing things. I got some cut rock in my car. Give you a nice buzz and keep the boogey man outta your dreams."

Dontay said, "The boogey man wasn't in my dreams. He was in my neighborhood."

Thump shoved Dontay against the wall. Hard. He said, "This is my neighborhood. My city."

Dontay felt his face go numb. He realized, after a face-to-face meeting with what he believed was death itself, Thump didn't scare him all that much.

"This thing," Dontay said. "Maybe this thing doesn't like you in *his* neighborhood."

Thump said, "Is this what happens when you start going to church? Word is you're there every day. You find you some Jesus?"

"It's a place to hang out," Dontay said.

"It's a place to hide," Thump said. "You can't hide from me."

Dontay felt his skin go cold. "You ain't the one I'm hiding from."

CHAPTER TWENTY

Totem pulled the piece of rubber tubing from his upper arm and allowed the chemicals that he had just injected himself with to begin to circulate. He had mixed them himself. Within about seven minutes he expected to achieve the perfect high. He had lit one small joint of some minor-grade weed and he had one glass of brandy from a bottle that he had spent nearly a hundred dollars on. He took one last puff of the joint and then lifted the brandy snifter to his nose. He gently blew the smoke into the glass and re-inhaled it, catching both the brandy and the weed in his nose as he sipped the deep red liquid. He set the brandy snifter down on the table next to his cell phone, which he had turned off. That would make Thump angry because he was supposed to be on call tonight, but he had been anxious to try his latest recipe—which included the weed, the brandy, the chemicals in his arm, and one good deep inhale from the black Sharpie marker he'd found in the kitchen but didn't remember buying. He sat back in his chair and allowed the ingredients to work together.

In his imagination, Totem believed when his spirit guide approached it would be a hawk and that it would take him flying and show him how to soar. He believed he would find himself in that limitless space. He knew this was wishful thinking. He knew that spirit guides appeared in whatever form they wanted and it had nothing to do with your personality. So if a lizard or a donkey showed up he knew not to be offended. Still, a hawk would be cool. He opened his eyes again and screamed like a junior high girl at a boy band concert. He put his hands on his cheeks and continued the long high-pitched note until he ran out of air.

The thing was on him in the next moment. It was twelve feet tall, twice his height. It put one oversized claw of a foot on each of the arm rests of his chair and squatted low so it could put their noses together. Totem tried not to be embarrassed. He had never heard of a spirit guide being a gargoyle but he supposed anything was possible.

"Spirit guide," Totem said. "Show me the way."

The black thing cocked its head to one side. Its gray forehead creased as if it was confused.

"Show me the way, O spirit guide," Totem said. His voice was shaking. He was wondering if this was such a good idea after all.

"This way," the thing said. It had a voice that sounded like it came from the bottom of a moldy well.

The thing backed off the chair and motioned for Totem to follow him.

* * *

Lois Bernhard was forty-eight years old. She had been a nurse since she was twenty-four—half of her life—had graduated at the top of her class, had led a nurse's strike six years ago, had been published multiple times in nursing magazines, and had published one well received but poorly selling book about the relationship between doctors and nurses. She had spent the previous two years in the maternity ward. She missed her daughter—rather, she missed her daughter being a baby. Babies are filled with wonder and then questions. Then they become teenagers and they get filled with anger and indifference and my-mom-is-sooooooo-stupid. Her daughter Padi—who for some unknown reason had decided to spell her name with a "d" instead of the two "t" and dot the "i" with a star—had been through so much and it finally seemed like she was coming out of a long dark tunnel.

When Padi's troubles started, Lois volunteered to move to floor seven. Fewer patients. Less stress. She only occasionally had to take the night shift. It was the floor for nurses' training. Out of nursing school and into the hospital—but for those first two weeks, the new nurses worked on floor seven. Half of floor seven was empty. There were computers in each room that responded to whatever input young nurses typed in at given intervals. They

*called these two weeks Hell Week because there
was little time for sleep, and it often seemed as if
the days ran together. The computer in room 701
was having a gallbladder operation. The computer
in room 702 had a broken leg. The computer in
room 703 was a woman who had kidney failure
and would die very soon. "Not die," Lois had told
a young nurse. "We call it negative treatment out-
come."*

*One more week of keeping these girls on their
toes in the middle of the night and she would be
done. They said many things about her behind her
back. Those most critical were the ones who would
not survive and did not belong as nurses. Most, she
thought, would be fairly competent nurses. Any
hospital would hire them. A few, she knew, could
go to work for one of the biggies in New York or at
the Cleveland Clinic if they continued to play their
cards right. There was one, every now and again,
whom she thought truly had a calling to be a nurse.*

*The word "bitch" had not bothered her for
years. Even patients freely used that one these days,
if they thought their aspirin was late or if their bed-
pan wasn't picked up quick enough. They would
call her names.*

*"Nurse Ratchet"—or "Rat-shit" as it was usual-
ly pronounced—just made her smile. Her favorite
phrase was something she had heard off a trainee
just a few weeks ago. One petite blonde nurse-in-
training who kept trying to hike up her white skirt
to show off her white hose had said, "She's seen it
all."*

Lois believed that she had. She had been there when the two-headed baby was born. The poor thing had only lived a few minutes but Lois had seen that the girls died in someone's arms and not in a cold sterile bed. She had been there when an entire girls' sorority had decided to "see what LSD is really like" and all of them had swallowed a grade of the drug that would have sent a Grateful Dead concert attendee into fits. Two of the girls died screaming in their rooms. Two suffered permanent damage. The others had eventually gone on to other adventures. Lois was in the emergency room when a kid named Thomas took his daddy's gun to school. She had seen births and deaths and one genuine miracle. Most things that patients and families considered miracles could be explained or at least theorized about. Lois had been there when a young priest had come to see a cancer patient. She had been outside the door when he put his hand on the little girl's forehead and wept along with her parents. Three days later the girl had been discharged from the hospital completely cancer-free.

Lois Bernhard had seen it all...or thought she had.

When the long-haired young man came flying through the window you could have knocked her over with a feather. The fact that she was on the seventh floor did not register in her mind until later. When the glass broke and the young man landed on floor she went into full nurse mode: help the patient, figure the rest out later—or try to. She would come up with all sorts of ideas but none of them would every truly satisfy her.

She hit the call button to summon a crash team, and knelt down beside the shivering man on the tile floor. He was cut from the glass, but nothing serious that she could tell. On his forehead someone had written, "Overdose" in black magic marker. The kid was out of his head and his eyes focused on nothing. He was babbling over and over, "Drugs are bad. Drugs are really, really bad. Really, really bad." He turned toward her and locked eyes. "Really, really, really bad," he said.

She said in her most calming voice, "Really, really bad. I know. Can you tell me what drugs you've taken?"

CHAPTER TWENTY-ONE

Thump put his phone back in his pocket after his 12th attempt to contact Totem. He didn't have a job for Totem at the moment, but there was some part of him that was genuinely concerned for his employee's welfare. If it turned out that Totem was on one of his spirit quests, Thump would just kick him in the kidneys later.

Thump looked out over the city from his favorite spot on the roof of the parking garage. This was his "office." Business was usually done in Mr. Cantrell's office but tonight was different. Tonight, Thump wanted to make a point. Thump had stood in Cantrell's office many times and watched as other managers had been dressed down for failures. He had escorted many applicants from the office. He had placed a heavy hand on many a shoulder, to simply let them know that the conversation was over and that Mr. Cantrell would like them to leave now.

Thump had never been in Councilman Moore's

office. He had driven Mr. Cantrell there once when he was an underling, so he knew where it was, but he had never been up there. Councilman Moore, who ran the PR agency that was responsible for how the rest of the country viewed Philadelphia— Councilman Moore who kept even the image of all things untidy away from the Liberty Bell— Councilman Moore who owned half of the buildings on the other side of the city away from the historic district—was fond of looking out of *his* office at *his* city as much as Thump enjoyed the roof of his parking deck.

Cantrell pulled up from the floor below and parked next to Thump. He liked to see how close he could pull up to where Thump was standing to see if he would make Thump move a step back and thereby make room for him. Thump had been reading a lot of business books lately. He had read a book called *Business Practices of The Samurai Warrior*, and knew that any step back was a sign of weakness. Cantrell knew this too, and didn't like that Thump had been reading the same book. He didn't like meeting in Thump's office and he didn't like coming out at night in this neighborhood.

"I hope you brought me out to tell me that you've solved your problem," Cantrell said as he walked around the front of the car.

"No," Thump said. "I brought you out to tell you that our problem is a little worse."

"You lost another one?"

"*We* lost the last two that we trust," Thump said.

"Get some more guys," Cantrell said.

"I don't have any that I can trust."

"You don't trust *any* of them," Cantrell said. Cantrell was shorter than Thump by a good foot and a half, but he had a large .357 that he liked to pull out of the back of his pants and wave around. Which is what did now. "You don't trust them. You give them incentive to do what they're told. Like not dying."

"We're losing customers too," Thump said, ignoring the fact that Cantrell was waving a pistol and would occasionally "accidentally" point it in his direction as he talked with his hands.

"What do you mean?"

"You watch the news? You read the papers?" Thump asked, annoyed.

"You mean the guy in the suit?" Cantrell said, laughing. "Some guy in an Acme Batman outfit beats up a few pushers and you think the whole city is scared?"

"I think," said Thump, "that someone is trying to rid the neighborhood of pushers and thieves. Customers aren't getting sent to the hospital. Customers are quitting and refusing to use your product. We lose customers, and our manufacturers find other places to go, and locations around this city go up for sale long before your boy in the glass building wants them to."

Cantrell stepped closer to Thump. "You think you're a businessman now?"

Thump said nothing.

"You think you can run this city? You *were* one

of those guys in the hospital now, until I brought you up to another level. You don't have the stones or the talent to take me on. I brought you up out of the street and I can put you back down there again." He tapped Thump's chest with the barrel of the .357. "I can put you under it."

Thump thought of his yoga breathing and made the conscious decision not to push Cantrell over the side of the garage. Instead, he looked out over the city.

Cantrell saw Thump's eyes go wide. He turned to see what his employee was gawking at. The two men stood on the top of the parking garage and placed their hands on the filthy concrete barrier and stood in amazement as a giant gargoyle with black wings and long trench coat floated out of the sky and landed on the roof of the church half a block down the street.

Cantrell turned to Thump and said, "Well, now you know where it lives. Lure it out...then kill it."

CHAPTER TWENTY-TWO

A STAR OVER THE I (EYE)
A blog about nothing, written for no one in particular, by someone who pretty much stopped giving a rat's ass about things a long time ago.

Entry: 665

My mom comes home and she's completely freaking.

I've been pacing back and forth in my room, making a path in the carpet and wondering if I should tell her what I saw the other night. I've been wondering if I should have said something to Rev. Dark, who apparently can do magic tricks with M&Ms. So I'm making a rut in the carpet and my mom bursts into the house. Mom does not "burst." Mom comes in slowly when it's late. She looks to see if my light is on. She comes in and sits on my bed and we have girl-talk, then she tells me not to stay up late. She does not burst. She used to burst. She used to get mad when I was up late. Now she doesn't. Really odd that my mom and I got close after my brief career as a criminal. Did you read that, Dr. Conners?

So mom bursts and starts telling me about a guy who overdosed on her floor. She's had stories before. Some boring. Some not so boring. None that made me want to become a nurse. Then she says, "Padi, it was on the 7th floor."

I say, "How did he come through the window on the 7th floor?"

She just stares at me. I told her it was like Bruce Willis in *Die Hard*. He was on rope or something and then swung down and crashed through the window. (Yippee Ky Yi Ya Motherfucker. Yes, you heard me. Watch the DVD sometime—it isn't Mellon Farmer.)

Mom says the guy was whacked out of his mind— there was no way he could have swung in.

I look at her and she says, "What?"

I keep looking at her and she says "What?" again and I know I'm about to get grounded. I tell her it was the big scary demon thing from the news. She says, "The nut job in the costume?"

I tell her it wasn't a guy in a costume. She says, how do I know? I tell her how I know and and we have a ten-minute argument about being where you are supposed to be when you are supposed to be there. Then we argue about whether or not I should be going back to that neighborhood. Then I tell her that the big scary demon thing ripped a guy out of his car who had just tried to sell drugs to her little girl. I tell her I ran a very long way and that I did not scream.

We look at each other for a long time. Then she says, "We will talk in the morning."

She goes to her room but she doesn't sleep. I can tell because I'm not asleep and I can hear her. She can probably hear me too. So we'll both sit in our room not sleeping and then we'll talk in the morning which is in like three hours.

CHAPTER TWENTY-THREE

There is no justice in this world. There is only bleak unfairness and a never-ending cycle of gray gloom.

Java Joe's does not open until eight on Sunday mornings.

I stood outside of Java Joe's with my hands and face pressed against the glass. I nearly cried.

The Right Reverend Lucas Haberkorn had graciously given up the 7am service to the new associate priest, who, because he was doing God's work the night before, overslept and found himself running through his apartment trying to find the little white thingy that fits into a clerical collar. It was in the freezer. Don't ask. I'm not entirely sure. See, when Bill Bixby turned into the Hulk, he had little or no memory of what he had done when *he* was a big scary beast. I am lucky enough to get to remember the look on certain people's faces...certain bad people who make noises like little girls before you throw them through the window of a hospital. Hey, it was a hospital. I hear he's going to be okay. Hanging outside the window I got to hear most of the "drugs are really, really bad" mantra. I think they should film that and play it in high schools across the country. We'd see a dramatic drop in teenage drug use. I'm learning that kids are pretty smart if you just be honest with them (spoken like a man who's been lying to his students since day one).

I threw myself out the door at 6:45 into the cold, cold, cold Philadelphia morning and was too intent on actually leading the service to see that the lights were off and the door was locked at Java Joe's. Dwight, how could you do this to me? There wasn't even time to get back up to my apartment and make a fresh pot of coffee. I was lost.

I remembered that Padi had told me the youth group had its own pop machine. She wasn't sure where it was. I checked the ring of keys that I had been given when I started (nearly a full week ago) and found that funky little round key that suggested caffeine salvation. I searched the ground floor and finally found the pop machine in a closet behind the kitchen. Of course, if you want to provide cold refreshing carbonated beverages to show the teenagers how much you truly appreciate them—you lock the machine in a closet. The machine wasn't even turned on, but the door opened. The cans all had expiration dates that dated back to when Padi attended nursery school here. Three warm expired Mountain Dews , and I was good to go. I was the new priest. I was the young guy in the collar, here to bring the word of God to the people of Philadelphia at seven o'clock in the morning.

I robed up. (Yes, a little secret there. That's what we call it...robing up.) I robed up and grabbed my Bible and Book of Common Prayer and stoically walked out into the sanctuary from behind the narthex and found my 7am congregation consisted of three people. Three people in a sanctuary that seats more than 500. You can't even lie about that to make yourself feel better. Everyone wanted a chance to meet and evaluate the new priest on board, but apparently they were all willing to wait until the 9am service to do it.

In the back of the room sat an older gentlemen in a suit and tie. The suit was pressed and clean, but he looked like he hadn't shaved the beard since that Mountain Dew I just drank was conceived.

In the front row sat Miss Roberta and Dontay. Miss Roberta was wearing her white gloves and a small pillbox hat with a large pearl-headed pin stabbed through what I hoped was hair. She sat with her small black imitation alligator vinyl bag in her lap clutching it with both hands as if someone might come along and yank it away from her. Dontay was asleep.

Miss Roberta smiled at me and waved just slightly as if she was in the center of a crowd. I felt like laughing. I don't know how many people regularly attend the 7am service on a good day. This one was gray outside and cold and was the kind of day when you really wanted to pull the covers up over your head and just worship the creator in your own private service. But like I said, three people. You can't really lie to yourself about that one.

I stood in the pulpit, feeling a little unworthy, and said, "Thou hast raised me from bed and sleep, O Lord; enlighten my mind and heart, and open my lips, that I may praise Thee, O Holy Trinity. Holy, Holy, Holy art Thou, O God. For the sake of the Mother of God, have mercy upon us."

Miss Roberta and the gentleman in the back responded with the proper Episcopal phrase: "Amen."

Dontay popped up and said, "Huh?" He looked up and saw me smiling at him and promptly went back to sleep on his grandmother's shoulder. I envied him.

I made it through my Morning Prayer service just fine. I knew Java Joe's would be open by the time I was done. I knew that in the 9am service I merely had to assist and not lead the service. I resigned myself to the notion that the hardest part of my day was over. (Yeah, you can sort of see that coming, can't you?)

Miss Roberta shook my hand and said, "Fine service, Reverend."

Dontay looked refreshed after his nap and I learned the gentleman in the back was Henry. Henry lived in what was called "homeless apartments" on 9th Street. It was a charity-owned building that allowed homeless folks to stay as long as they wanted. If they were caught with alcohol or were arrested for any reason they were out. Mr.

Henry Davis had lived there for nine years. He had one suit that he kept in impeccable condition and spent most of his days looking for recyclables and begging for change. He shook my hand, and I thought I saw him smile from beneath the extensive beard, but I could not tell. He pulled the suit coat a little closer around him and ventured out into the morning without a word.

I told myself the 9am service would be better.

* * *

It truly is a wonderful sight to see when young people gather in the name of Jesus to sing praises and to pray together. This group of twelve young men, none over the age of twenty-one, sat in the back two rows and created a presence in that room that you could almost taste. They all wore the black hooded sweatshirts that gangs wear to funerals. The message was not lost. Somebody knew something.

None of them were aware of proper church posture. They slouched. Some of them even put their feet up on the pew in front of them—much to the dismay of several long time members.)

In a mostly white, mostly happy, mostly upper-middle-class congregation, these guys were here for a reason. I will give them this, they didn't seem to have a race restriction on their membership rolls. Equal opportunity intimidators.

These were young men who spent an inordinate amount of time practicing a look that said, "I eat small children."

Long-time, you're-sitting-in-my-pew members decided to worship God from a new vantage point. A large crowd had been expected anyway. Everyone was going to show up and make predictions about the new minister. The crew of twelve (which, by the way, is how Jesus referred to the disciples. No, I made that up. Sucker.) took up the back two rows, and the rest of the congregation crammed themselves into three quarters of the room, giving these new potential members as much space as they could. Imagine, if you will, that you just opened a half-gallon rectangular carton of really vanilla ice cream and then scooped the lower right-hand corner out—leaving the rest of it smooth and perfect and hard-packed and vanilla. This is what the sanctuary looked like on my first Sunday.

Lucas and I stood in the back in our robes, looking at the congregation, trying to not look at the new arrivals, all at the same time. There were glances, dropped pencils, and coughs, followed by a quick peep toward the back rows.

"Friends of yours?" Lucas asked.

I looked at him to see if he was kidding. He seemed to be. This was a man who had been a servant for nearly fifty years. I doubted there was much he hadn't seen. He had the look of someone who didn't let a lot upset him in the church while others could throw a hissy fit inside their own skin.

"You wanted me to expand the youth group," I said. He smiled and the organ started to play. Lucas and I took our spots behind the choir as we processed in behind the cross. Everyone stood. The gentlemen in the back waited five seconds after everyone else hit their feet to let people know that standing was something *they* decided to do, and not because anyone told them to. It was all about attitude. Intimidation is 90% attitude. It can get you places, trust me.

In the front row, in the same spot as before, sat Miss Roberta and Dontay. I looked quizzically at her, and she just smiled. I guess some people go to the movies. Miss Roberta comes to church. There was a big difference in Dontay. No longer willing to drift off to sleep on his grandmother's shoulder, Dontay sat straight. He sat as still as a statue, except for his eyes. He kept trying to look behind him at the back row without actually turning his head. He was sweating bullets.

In the Episcopal Church they "pass the peace." This is three minutes during the service where they walk around, shake hands (or hug), and someone says, "Peace be with you," and the proper response is "And also with you." Let's try it. You and me.

"Peace be with you."

"_____"

Now would that have killed you to say it out loud? During the service, Rev. Haberkorn announced the Passing of the Peace and people began milling about passing and responding. No one ventured toward the back quarter of the sanctuary to where the group of young men had already resumed their seated and slouching positions. It was that I'm-too-tired-to-deal-with-you-right-now-pose that Dontay had shown me when I first met him. I mean when I met him as Michael. You know what I mean.

I shook several hands of several nice people who all wanted to show me how welcome I was. Rev. Haberkorn nudged me and nodded toward the back.

Dorothy, in all of her five-foot-two polyester glory, had ventured back and was hugging each of the gang bangers individually. She was smiling as if she hadn't seen these old friends in years. I had a brief picture of Dorothy as a gang-banger and it made me smile. In spite of themselves, these guys each stood up and received his special hug. I looked back at Lucas, and he was trying not to laugh. Dorothy finished hugging all of the men in black, and then promptly sat down in the middle of them. She pulled out the Book of Common Prayer and began teaching a lesson for the uninitiated in how it worked. I had seen this move before. Some guy years ago who came and sat with a bunch of us as we were drinking and swearing and trying to talk a girl named Rebecca out of her robes. Christ, Dorothy was being Christ.

I caught a quick glimpse of Padi on the far side. She smiled and flashed me the peace sign. I guess it was the Episcopalian version. I scanned the balcony and spotted another familiar face. It was Susan. You've heard the expression "sweating like a whore in church." Susan looked uncomfortable, but it wasn't because of where she was. She didn't' take her eyes off the group beneath her. She had seen them before. She knew something.

CHAPTER TWENTY-FOUR

After the eleven o'clock service everyone gathered in Howver Hall, named in memory of a long time high-donation member. There were donuts and coffee and small children who got underfoot simply because they had just sat semi-still for an hour and now had been properly sugared.

I was standing, now in shirt and collar, among a group of white haired women and several soccer moms who had been told the new priest was single.

Haberkorn touched my elbow and said, "See you in my office when you have a chance." I mingled, and a few minutes later made my way out of the hall with a cup of rancid church coffee in a Styrofoam cup. Someday churches will get the idea that the money they spend on cheap flyers and "Come visit us" post cards would be much better spent on better coffee. Show me a church that knows how to run a cappuccino maker, and I'll show you a church that will be building a family life center in five years.

I knocked and he invited me in. On his desk were two glasses of wine. He handed me one and said, "This is better than the coffee." He sat down at his desk chair and put his feet up on desk. I set my cup down on the filing cabinet and relaxed in the chair across from him.

"So," he said, "I thought it went really well."

I agreed.

"Did we have the same visitors in the early service?"

I said they would have outnumbered the rest of the congregation. He nodded knowingly. "I wonder what they wanted?"

"Not sure," I said. "Though it did seem to be a message."

"Your expertise in youth ministry doesn't give you any clue?"

Expertise. He was funny. I said, "Well, you know Dontay? Roberta Park's grandson?"

He nodded. "Just by his picture. I think I met him when he was a youngster. How old is he now?"

"Fifteen or sixteen," I said. "I think he was involved in something and got out recently. It might be connected."

He sipped his wine. "So you're thinking Dontay was fulfilling the stewardship goal and invited some of his friends to join us in worship?" He smiled over the rim of his glass at me.

"I'm not at all sure of what was going on there," I lied. I had an idea of the why but I didn't know the how.

He started to giggle. I said, "What?"

He giggled a little more and started to shake.

I said, "What? What?"

He rubbed his ancient eyes and said, "Did you see the look on their faces when Dorothy went over and started hugging them?"

I laughed too. "She was fearless, wasn't she?"

"I'm sure you've heard the story of the child molester by now."

I nodded. "Two versions."

He drained his glass and said, "When it gets up to four, let me know and I'll fill you in."

He straightened up in his chair and I took that as a "thanks for coming" motion. I finished my glass and stood. He said, "I'm also not planning on retiring anytime soon."

I caught his meaning and put my hand on his shoulder. "Lucas, I'm not your replacement. No one ever said anything like that to me. I'm here because I was sent here and because you believe in a God of second chances. That's it."

He seemed to believe it. It never occurred to me that Lucas might think I was part of a conspiracy to force him out. I started to leave and he said, "There's one more thing."

I took my hand off the doorknob and he said, "There was a young woman in the balcony. I'm pretty sure I've seen her around before but never here in church. She kept watching you and watching the gang-bangers. Is there anything I should know?"

I turned and said, "I slept in my car the night I

arrived. The young lady offered me her services and I declined. I saw her in the coffee shop and invited her to church. I never in a million years thought she'd show up. She may be familiar with our guests, but I don't know how and I don't know why they were here. That's really all there is to it, Lucas."

He nodded. I felt like a schmuck for lying to him. But that was the way it worked sometimes. In my apartment I switched to jeans and a T-shirt with a picture of Jesus riding a raptor. I put on the warm jacket that had appeared in my luggage when I arrived, and headed out into the cold Philadelphia autumn. I thought maybe I'd walk down to the Terminal and get a cheese steak or try out Gino's and see if they were better or not. Outside the church I saw a familiar face through the window at Java Joe's. Lunch plans change.

Joe had just added a pumpkin latte to the list. I stood in line and ordered one of those with one of his mammoth muffins, hoping I might get to eat this one.

I walked over to where Susan was sitting and said, "I saw you in church. Do you mind if I sit down?"

She gave me a half-smile and I took that as a yes.

I said, "Look, I'll put the invitation out there again..."

She immediately interrupted me with, "I think I saw Satan and he saved my life. Does that mean I'm going to hell?"

Whoa. I said, "Look there's a lot of different ideas about what Satan is."

She said, "Satan is 12 feet tall, has black wings, and a voice that sounds like a garbage disposal."

"Ah," I said. She sounded so sure of herself. It had been a long time since I had looked into a mirror when I was...well...the other one.

"I think," I began, "that if Satan wanted to take you to hell he would have done it. He wouldn't have saved your life. Maybe it wasn't Satan. A lot of people are talking about that big guy in the costume..."

"I saw it," she said. "I saw it, I heard it."

"What did it say to you?"

"It didn't talk to me, but it talked to my pimp as he was getting the shit kicked out of him."

I nodded. "You know, Satan was one of God's angels," I offered. "Maybe they don't all have the big fluffy wings. If some guy in a white robe and fluffy wings had shown up what would have happened?"

She almost smiled. "My pimp would have beat the hell out of him."

Ahhh, irony. "Okay, then," I said, "let's rule out Satan and say it was just a big scary angel."

"Does God do that?" she asked.

"What?"

"Make angels that are big and scary?"

"Well, I think God will do whatever God wants to do, and when it comes down to it we don't have a clue as to what's involved in that. So, I'm willing to make that leap if you are."

She was quiet. She started to speak once—twice—and then sat back and sighed.

"Okay then," I said, "let's say that God sent a big scary angel to beat up your pimp. Sounds like God was punishing him, not you."

"But I deserved it, too."

"Why?"

"'Cause I'm not exactly a nun."

I conceded that point. "But," I said, "it would seem you've been give a reprieve of sorts. A second chance. Maybe God wants you to try a different line of work."

"Yeah, I'll see if schoolteacher is still open."

"God loves everyone," I said. "Even those who really don't deserve it." I was speaking from experience on this one. "We call that grace."

"He didn't seem to be loving Naws," Susan said.

"Lets call that tough love," I offered.

"I don't understand."

"Neither do I," I said. "But I know that God loves me. He gave me a pass a *long* time ago, and so everyday I try to be the kind of person who deserves that kind of grace."

She sat there mulling that one over.

"I wanted to ask you about the gentlemen who came to church this morning."

"Are you into something bad, Father?" she asked.

"You're the second person today who has asked me that," I said. "Do I have that kind of face?"

Susan said, "I know those guys. I know who they work for. I know they don't go out on social calls and they really don't go to church. They were sent there. Somebody sent them as a message to some-one at the church."

"Who do they work for?" I asked.

"Father, you don't want in on that."

"It appears I'm already in on that," I said. "Who do they work for?"

"They work for a guy named Thump. He works for Cantrell. Everybody works for Cantrell. If those guys were there and Thump sent them, it's because Cantrell told him to."

I could see her hands starting to shake while they were holding her cup.

"What does Cantrell want?" I asked.

"Cantrell wants everything," she said. "If he can't make you give it to him he'll take it. If you tell him he can't have it, he'll steal it. If you try to stand in his way, he'll just kill you."

"What would he want at Saint Marjorie's?"

"Who knows?" she said. "Either somebody has something he wants, or he was trying to scare somebody."

"What if I went and saw him?"

Her eyes got really wide. "What, you have a death wish or something?"

"I can go talk to him. I don't like games. If he just told me what he's after, then maybe we can come to some sort of agreement and he'll just leave us all alone."

She actually laughed at me. "Cantrell doesn't leave anybody alone."

"Suppose I talk to this man Cantrell."

"You really are crazy aren't you?"

"I don't like drugs," I said. "I don't like people ruining other people's lives. I have too much experience with that. There's a young man in my church. He just started coming. I think he was one of Cantrell's customers and now he isn't anymore. Now he's in my house and I want Mr. Thump and Mr. Cantrell to leave him alone."

"Sounds too small," she said. "I don't think he'd send 12 guys to intimidate one kid when just one big guy would do. It must be something else."

I didn't want to think about that. I wanted to make sure Dontay was safe and that Susan was safe. One of the things I had missed out on, when I was—as they say—alive originally, was the idea of actually caring about someone. As a guardian...it came with the territory. Gabriel once told me that I had the ability to care about people when I was alive too, and that I just chose to ignore it. I told him he was full of crap.

"Are you okay?" I asked. "Do you need some money?"

"I've got some," she said.

"Are they going to come after you if you don't...report for work?"

She half-smiled. "Thanks for putting it that way. No, I don't think so. The only one I'd worry about was Naws, and he hasn't been around."

I could swear I saw her smirk for just a moment. I knew she was thinking about Naw's "apology." Guys, it's the little things that make your woman happy. Remember that.

"Tell me about Cantrell," I said.

She said, "You can't change anything."

"I'm just going to ask him to leave this kid I know alone. That's all. Then I'll be done."

"You'll be lucky if he doesn't have Thump rip your arm off and beat you with it till you go away."

"I'll take my chances."

She said, "Thump hangs out on the roof of the parking garage near your church. He likes it up there at night. Cantrell, he has an office."

"What do you mean, an office?" I asked.

"There's a tattoo place on 18th. The second floor is Cantrell's office, but he keeps all his records someplace else."

"Must be difficult for his secretary," I said.

She looked at me. "Was that a joke?"

"Sorta."

"Father, this man is into everything. Drugs, mostly; prostitutes. He says he's going to go into real estate next. Naws was going to take over the girls, but I don't think that's going to happen now."

"Because of the...obstacle." I offered.

"Because of the big fucking demon that tried to eat him," she blurted without batting an eye. A few people in the shop looked over at us. I was hoping there was no one there from the congregation. I was really starting to like her.

"Probably not my choice of words," I said. "But yeah. Because of that."

"Father, you came to town at the wrong time."

"Or maybe the right one."

"You really don't want to do this, Father," she

said, but when she looked out the window I got the clear sense that she desperately needed me to.

"Promise me you'll stick around for awhile," I said. "Things might change. I'm sure there's something we can work out."

"Why are you being nice to me?" she asked.

"I'm nice to pretty much everyone," I lied. It was only a partial lie. I wasn't all that nice to Naws the other night, but I think that was sort of a retroactive niceness to her. So I counted it.

"People aren't nice to people like me unless they want something," she said.

"I know the feeling," I told her. That took a minute but she smiled again.

"Stick around," I said. I got up to leave, and just as I went out the door I met Henry Davis coming in. Henry had changed out of his suit and into his "working clothes." Jeans, shirt, shoes, and a coat that looked like he'd slept in a puddle. Which he may have, before he got the apartment.

"Spare a dollar for breakfast, Father?"

I handed him the bag with the muffin and he walked the other way. One of these days I really wanted to try one of those.

CHAPTER TWENTY-FIVE

It occurred to me that I had not been out of the church without my own "working clothes" (if you will) at night since arriving in this city. I felt strangely naked.

I stood on the top floor of the parking garage just down the street from the church. There were eight floors. The seventh was under some sort of construction and the roof was blocked off. I had to really go all out to outwit the security procedures by moving the orange cone. At least when the door was opened at Saint Marjorie's, a small light flashed above the secretary's desk. Alice would know someone was in the building—God help the rest of us.

I stood in my priestly attire in the center of the roof. I looked as out of place as…well I was going to say "as a whore in church" but technically that's not correct as the Son of God invited all the wrong people to church all the time.

I looked as out of place as a loaf of Wonder Bread at that wonderful deli that Rev. Haberkorn had taken me to.

If this was Thump's office then he would have to show up eventually. What kind of a name was Thump? Back in my day, we had Goliath and Maximus. "Thump" was the sound his head was going to make if I decided to relieve him of it. I stood there thinking about fear. So many people let fear run their lives whether they are aware of it or not. They are afraid of being alone. They are afraid of pain. They are afraid of the dark. They are afraid of death.

Most fears go back to the fear of the unknown. We fear being alone because we don't know what's going to happen. We fear pain because we don't know what do to or how to react. We fear the dark because we don't know what's there. Ultimately, we fear death because (even with all those hymns) people don't know what happens next. Fear of the unknown. That's what keeps most people in line.

I mention this because there is no unknown for me. I know what happens after you close your eyes for the last time (or have someone close them for you). I'm not afraid of that, not anymore. This poses a problem for those who rule through fear and intimidation. I'm just not afraid.

I stood there with a Bible in my hands. It was old. Leather cover. Well worn. The kind a priest would carry. When I was 12, it took two of us to carry the Torah from where it was stored to the stand where it would be read. The Bible may have a few of its facts back-assward but at least it's compact. Gabriel had put this one in my bag with the other stuff. I've read it a few times. Some of it's familiar. Some, it's like your mother telling you the things you did as a child, and if you really stretch you might be able to just barely place a memory on what she's talking about.

I held the Bible to my face and smelled the cover. Gabriel's attention to detail was amazing sometimes. The pages smelled old but the leather cover still smelled nice. I saw the light behind me and I knew he was there.

"You know, sometimes, I do like your work," I said as I turned around to greet one of God's favorites. (What do you call a teacher's pet when the teacher is the creator of all things?) Pay a guy a compliment and you'd think you might actually get a smile or something.

"Are you playing nice?" he asked. He actually had a glowing clipboard with him. I could have gotten one of those things at Office Max and here he was using it to look angelic. His white robe hung below his feet, but it still did not touch the dirty concrete beneath mine. He was always just a little too good for the rest of us.

"I'm playing nice," I said.

"You put several people in the hospital." He didn't look up from his notes.

"I didn't kill anyone," I protested. Yeah, that made him look up.

"There are rules," he said.

"Don't you think that when I came on board the rules changed a little? I'm a special case. I have different gifts. You don't think that gives me a get-out-of-regular-gym pass?"

"I'm saying," he said—he had stopped writing to look at me—"that you live so close to the edge, so much, that you don't leave yourself room. You know you can only go so far. If you push it all the time, what happens when you want to go just a little more?"

"We'll find out, won't we?" Yeah, that's me. King of the comebacks.

"You are here to watch over. You're getting too directly involved."

"I'm watching over," I protested.

"You turned over a car and beat a man into the hospital. Several of them."

"The one guy was beating a woman."

"The others?"

"Selling drugs to kids and other living things."

"That's not exactly playing nice."

"What are you going to do?" I asked. "Stand me in the corner? Send me to bed without supper."

He didn't even try to look menacing. He just said, "I could. You know I could."

"Don't you think that playing nice may not be what He wants on this one?" I asked. I waved the Bible at him so he could know which "He" I was referring to.

"A bully is always a bully," he said.

I said, "Yeah, you're right. Only in this case, you have a bully that's going to take the lunch money back from other bullies. That doesn't make him the head of the class."

"Still, if he gets caught fighting he gets suspended," Gabriel said.

"Do you think we could ditch the schoolyard analogies?" I asked. Gabriel became an empty space. He had made his point. I took a deep breath and resigned myself to the fact that Thump's head would remain on his shoulders. For now, at least.

CHAPTER TWENTY-SIX

**A Brief Interlude To Tell You
Something That Happened About Six Years Ago**

Tony Robertson had been expelled from Philadelphia University during his sophomore year (there was a little irony in that Tony had been expelled from high school during his sophomore year for precisely the same crime, which he committed for precisely the same reason). Actually, in high school he had been given in-school suspension the first three times but when you are a computer hacker and don't get a chance to date all that much and exactly one-half of the cheerleading squad is failing math, you might just be willing to risk getting caught a third time.

At the Philadelphia University, Tony excelled in all his classes and even created a new software for tracking alumni who moved out of state. The girl's name was Rachel and she wasn't a cheerleader, but she was a flag girl in the marching band. Tony had a thing for short skirts.

She was failing Introduction To American Economics, and went to Tony for tutoring. Tony suggested they could both save time. Tony also knew that Intro to American Economics meant she'd be back next year.

Tony changed her grade and got caught. This time Tony did not rat the young woman out. The University Board of Conduct told Tony they could have him arrested in addition to having him expelled. Tony pleaded his case and the board decided they would simply expel him if he promised to give them the software he created to track alumni. Tony agreed, but not before adding in a small glitch that would call the University President on the 18th of every month and emit an ear piercing siren at 1:37am.

The Board of Conduct consisted of three faculty members, two student government majors, and two prominent members of the community: Marvin Oestriecher, who owned and operated seven donut shops in the area (each one called Palcho's), and Councilman Chris Moore who was also into real estate.

After the initial hearing the Councilman came up to Tony and said, "How would you like a job?"

CHAPTER TWENTY-SEVEN

I knew a man named Seth. He went to Ethiopia (back then, we called it Abyssinia). He came back a year later with some great stories and a tattoo that was more intricate than anything I've seen here...ever. It started under his hairline and wove its way down in an intricate pattern of snake and lizard in front of his ear, then it disappeared down his cloak and poked out of his sleeve where his two middle fingers when held together had the dark black image of a knife.

He said it had taken the artist an entire year to complete. Apparently there was more of it that the rest of us never asked to see.

Thump's tattoo was almost that good (less intricate. I doubt Mr. Thump would have had the patience to sit still every day for a year while the artist worked on it). His covered the side of his head. There were a lot of points, like barbed wire the size of your fist. One sharp edge jutted out over his eye. The rest, a deep black series of jagged edges, disappeared under his black hooded sweat-shirt.

He was big. Screw that, he was a tank in a black sweatshirt. He had dreads but he kept them hidden under the hood which he pulled over his head. You had to look up to see his eyes, because he was also at least six foot six. He stood in front of the tattoo shop. It was called Inkwell, which I thought was rather clever. People had been staring at me for the last seven blocks. Once you hit a certain point in this city, you become something of an anomaly. I think it was the collar.

People would pass by me and I could feel their eyes as they turned around to question whether or not they had just seen a priest walk by. I stopped a moment to smell the smoke coming from an air vent in an alley. It was lamb. I used to love lamb.

I saw the shop. I saw the very large man standing in front of the door that led to the second floor. He seemed to get bigger the closer I got to him, and I don't mean as a trick of perspective. The man was very large. He didn't see me until I was just across the street. Even behind the sunglasses I could see his brows crease. To him I might as well have been wearing on of those big character costumes you see the amusement parks.

I walked right up to him and looked up into this hood. I extended my hand, and before he realized what he was doing (too caught up in the moment, I suppose) he put his out as well. "Are you Mr. Thump?" I asked, my voice now sounding like an insurance commercial.

"Yes," he said. He had his composure back now but his moment of intimidation was gone. I had caught him off guard and he would spend the next part of the conversation trying to get it back. He had that whole fear thing going but I had startled him. It was going to take a lot more to intimidate me.

I said, "Father Michael Dark of Saint Marjorie's. Do you know our church?"

He stared at me. He was getting that menacing face back again. He said, "Are you ...(he wanted to say "insane") lost?"

"No." I smiled. "I wanted to take a minute to talk to Mr. Cantrell, and I understand you are the man to take me to see him."

Thump, fully back in control now, said, "I don't know any one by that...."

I pushed ahead. "Mr. Cantrell sent some visitors to our church this past Sunday and I wanted to be sure and thank him and invite him to come and be a part of our worship service as well."

There was a time when a man did his business in the cave. You put your biggest guy at the entrance and if a Roman soldier came up you simply "shared the wealth" and he went away. If someone who had no business there came up and wouldn't go away...he simply disappeared. Your man at the entrance to the cave had to be trusted. He also had to be discreet. This was a velvet rope bouncer with an attitude and a short sword.

Thump? Well, he was good. Like I said, he had the intimidation thing down but he lacked something in the follow-through. The next thing I knew he was leading me up a set of stairs that smelled like a urinal and into a short hallway with just two doors. Neither was labeled. Thump knocked twice and led me into Cantrell's office.

Cantrell was a wiry guy. Too much coke or way too much caffeine, I'm not sure which. He was on the phone when we went in. He seemed so surprised that Thump would actually bring me into the office that he simply hung up without saying goodbye. A collar certainly brings out the best in people.

"Thump?" he said, looking at his doorman as if he was already pondering a staff change.

Before Thump could start speaking, I extended my hand and said, "Mr. Cantrell. I'm Rev. Michael Dark from Saint Marjorie's Cathedral downtown. I apologize for not making an appointment. I know you're a busy man." He shook my hand and gave me the same look that Thump had given me downstairs. It was a look that said, "Are you an idiot or a complete asshole?"

Without being asked, I sat down in the leather chair across from his desk.

The room was a hole. No carpeting. Wallpaper from the 50's when the building was built. I doubted it was a tattoo shop then. The desk, however, was mahogany. Easily several grand in the desk and in each chair. His was large and high backed. There were two pieces of art in his office. One on each wall. The first was an oil painting of a red-headed woman reclining naked across a bed of satin sheets.

The satin covered her nether regions but both breasts were freely exposed and she seemed to be taking a great interest in the taste of her little finger. The other was a modern art piece that I guessed Mr. Cantrell had purchased because it was expensive and because someone had told him that all business men have expensive unexplainable art in their office.

He said down and said, "Reverend, I don't keep a lot of cash here in the office. I'm not sure what sort of donation you're collecting for, but..."

I interrupted. "No, no. I'm afraid you misunderstood me. I apologize. I understand that you and your associate here sent some visitors to our church last Sunday and I wanted to come by and personally thank you for extending that invitation to the community. I know you do a lot with underprivileged youth."

He immediately tried to get back control of the situation. He looked at me. The lower half of his face smiled but his eyes narrowed in a way that told me he knew I was jerking him around.

"Reverend, you don't impress me as a man who beats around the bush. So let us cut the bullshit, shall we?"

I nodded. "That would be easier and move things along, wouldn't it?"

"What can I do for you?"

I said, "I'd like you and all of your associates to leave a student of mine alone. His name is Dontay. He's a good kid. He's trying to find the right path. I want him left alone."

His smile widened. He actually thought that was funny. He looked at Thump, who had not left my shoulder, and then back at me. "I'm sorry. Who did you say you wanted me to leave alone? I'm afraid you have me confused with someone else."

"I thought you wanted to cut the bullshit," I said. "I know what you deal and how you deal. You're an amateur compared to what I've seen in my lifetime. You don't have the first clue as to how to really run a city from the underside. Now, I've asked you to leave my student alone. One kid failing to give you the money he took out his grandmother's purse is not going to affect your..."—I gestured toward his walls with the opposing artwork—"business."

We looked at each other. I was thinking he had read one of those *Way of The Samurai* business books and was thinking that I was trying to hold his eye contact in a show of who had the bigger "desk."

I smiled and allowed him to win. Standing, I said, "It was a pleasure to make your acquaintance." I held out my hand to Thump. "And yours too, Mr. Thump." The large man did not take it, but I did see his eyes start to smoke. "Well then, I'm off. Gentlemen, please feel free to stop and worship with us any Sunday. I'll show myself out." I walked toward the door. I was really hoping that Gabriel was watching. Did I really think it was over? No.

Was I deliberately provoking them? Kind of.

Did I think they would leave Dontay alone? No, I did not really think that. I did think they might lighten up a little, at least give him a chance, because dealing with me would not be worth the hassle.

Did I feel responsible for what they did to him after that? Yes, I did.

I still do.

* * *

I walked into my office at three o'clock. I had three large coffees and a bag of Dwight's chocolate chip cookies. Padi was in her usual spot, probably trying to hack into NASA from my computer. Dontay was sitting in one of the guest chairs, reading a comic book with a zombie on the cover.

I sat next to him and said, "Did you know there are zombies in the Bible?"

He looked at me and then over at Padi. His eyes were clearer now then I had ever seen them. He seemed like whatever had been running through his system had finally worked its way out. Padi said to Dontay, "He means Jesus rising from the dead. He's trying to pull a Jesus lesson on you."

Dontay looked at me and then began reading again. I handed him a coffee. "*Buuuzzzzzzzzz,*" I said. "I'm sorry, that's incorrect, but thanks for playing our game."

Now Dontay looked up at me again and Padi turned in her, or rather *my*, chair to face me. I had them. "All right," she said, "Go ahead."

"Grab that Bible," I said to Dontay who reached

behind him to the bookshelf and took down a red leather edition. A King James Version. Classy.

I said, "You know how to work it?"

He nodded. "My grandma showed me."

"Good," I said, "Look up Matthew 27:52-53"

He did and he read it out loud for Padi, "And the graves were opened; and many bodies of the saints which slept arose, and came out of the graves after his resurrection, and went into the holy city, and appeared unto many."

"So," Padi said. "Doesn't call them zombies. Doesn't say they were walking around all drippy with parts falling off."

"Doesn't say they weren't," I said. "There's a whole army of zombies in Ezekiel. Can you find that one?"

Dontay started flipping pages. He said, "You really think they were like zombies?"

"I wasn't there," I said, which was true. I was close but not there. I said to Dontay, "There's a lot of stories about Jesus or one of the disciples raising somebody from the dead, but this is the only place where it talks about graves opening and dead people in mass quantities wandering into town. Sounded like a George Romero movie to me."

"Show me another one," Dontay said. He was grinning like a 12-year-old who had just come across a secret stash of *Playboys* hidden in the woods.

The phone on my desk beeped loudly, and Alice's voice blared through the speaker. I had no idea the

phone could do that. "Reverend Dark." She sounded bothered.

"Yes?" I said to the phone.

"You have a visitor."

"Really?" I was surprised. "Who is it?"

Alice paused for dramatic effect and then in a
louder voice, which I'm sure was meant to be heard
by others in the lobby area. "It's a Detective
Maggie Grafton with the Philadelphia police,"
Alice said.

Both Padi and Dontay looked at me and then at
each other and then at the phone. I decided to play
it cool. "Thank you, Alice. Please tell the detective
I'll be right down."

There was an audible click and then we were
alone in the silence, still looking at the phone.
Dontay said, "Busted" under his breath.

I stood up and said to Padi, "Are you really as
good as you say you are, or do you just put on a
good show with that thing?" I pointed at my computer. "Can you find any information you want?"

"Pretty much," she said. "Except for launch
codes. That might take me an hour."

"Can it be traced back to this computer?"

"No," she said. "I set you up with a dummy
account at fotspot.com last week."

I had no idea what that meant but I assumed she
was good at what she did. "There's a tattoo place
called Inkwell," I said. "Can you find out who
owns that building?"

"Cost you another coffee tomorrow."

"Done."

"And one for my research assistant." Dontay looked at me. He had whipped cream on his upper lip.

"Do you know how much a latte costs?" I asked.

"Do you even know how to turn your computer on?" she asked.

"Mocha or caramel?" I asked.

* * *

Detective Maggie Grafton of the Philadelphia police department was one the most striking women I had ever met. When I arrived in the lobby, she was twirling a stocking cap on her finger. She had red hair, the kind that seems like it gets curly when it gets wet, and it had been doing one of those misty rains all day, so she had lots of red curls which she had tried to pull together behind her head. She was staring a picture of the church congregation taken in 1957. It was one of the earliest photographs the church had.

"Detective?" I said.

When she turned to face me her coat opened slightly and I could see the gun and holster, and I suddenly remembered that this woman could probably drop a man in an instant. She had probably had to shoot someone at some time. She more than likely had stared down the wrong end of the barrel. She had seen a lot more death and waste of life than I had and I instantly felt like a schmuck for checking her out when I got off the elevator.

"Reverend Dark," she said, all business, her

handshake firm. No doubt a trick learned for dealing with idiots like me who didn't see past the hair and the eyes on the first meeting.

"Is there someplace we can talk privately?" she asked. I could feel Alice's eyes on my back as I positioned myself between the detective and the secretary.

"Of course," I said. "I have students in my office at the moment, but we can talk in the sanctuary. It's empty right now."

I put my hand lightly on her back and gestured her down the hall. We passed Rev. Haberkorn's office (he was not in) and arrived at the big double doors to the Sanctuary.

I love an empty sanctuary. I realize that's blasphemous if you are sitting on the treasury committee of a large church like this one, but I love the silence of a big room. I love the stained glass windows in the afternoon. If all you ever do is show up on a Sunday morning, you should go visit a church at other times. The room is constantly changing with light beams and shadows. We walked in. The sun (usually behind a thin gray cloud at this time of year) had poked through and put a large shaft of orange-red-yellow light on the pews.

She said, "I used to come here when I was a little girl. When did you start working here?"

"'Bout a week ago," I said.

She said, "Ahhh," as if that explained something.

"What is it I can do for you, Detective?"

"You can call me Maggie," she said. She was lost in some memory from years ago. "I remember this church on Christmas Eve. That was always my favorite service."

"Why did you stop coming?" I asked. "If you don't mind my asking."

"Parents divorced. I went to college. The academy. I got lazy and God pissed me off."

"Well, that's honest," I said.

She sat down in a pew and I took the one directly in front of her, turning around so we could talk. She was still looking at the windows.

"It's okay to be pissed off at God," I said. "Lots of people are. The Jewish people think it's healthy. Clears the air. It's when you stop believing altogether that things get dicey."

She suddenly came back to herself, if you will, and stopped twirling the hat on her finger. "Reverend, you paid a visit today to the second floor of a tattoo shop. Do you mind if I ask you what you were doing there?"

"You were watching me?"

"We were watching the tattoo shop," she said, "We have been for awhile. Today you stopped by. You'd never been there before."

I played it honest. "I have a student who is trying to put his life back together before it gets too broken to fix. I asked around. I heard that Mr. Cantrell on the second floor would be the man to talk to in that area."

"You just walked in and asked him to quit selling to one of your students?" She gave me the same look that Cantrell and Thump had. What is it with these people?

"Yes," I said. "I asked him to leave my student alone and then I left."

"Did he answer you?"

"Not in so many words," I said.

"What were the exact words?"

"His exact words were, 'I think you have me confused with someone else.'"

"So he never actually admitted to selling your student anything, or suggested that he had instructed anyone else to?" she asked.

"By 'anyone else,' do you mean the larger man-mountain he keeps at his door?"

"Him," she said, "or any of his distributors who have spent the better part of the week in the hospital."

"Those men work for Cantrell?" I asked innocently.

"Everybody works for Cantrell," she said.

"Except the police department," I said.

She looked at me with a don't-be-naïve look "Reverend," she started.

"Michael," I said.

"Okay," she said. "Michael. I don't know where you came from, but at some point you must have wondered if that was a good idea."

"Honestly, it didn't occur to me."

"It should have," she said. "You may already be in deeper than you want to be for the new guy in a cushy job."

"Cushy." I repeated the word.

"I'm being honest with you," she said, "This can't be that hard a gig. You either have friends in high places or you're being groomed for something else. Nobody your age gets this kind of assignment."

"Well," I said, "I think the friends-in-high-places thing goes without saying."

She didn't smile.

"And," I offered, "I got this job because I was assigned to it. If I'm 'being groomed' as you put it, then it's happening without my knowledge. I have a kid who's standing on the ledge between backing up on the roof and stepping off into oblivion. I thought I would take my concerns directly to the source."

"And who told you Cantrell was the source?"

"A hooker," I said.

She didn't flinch, even though I expected her too.

"Reverend, listen to me on this one. I grew up in this city. You don't want to mess around outside of the historical district. Spend some time taking your young people to the museums. Teach them about civic duty. But stay away from their dealers. It's bad news."

"I was really hoping this conversation would go differently," I said.

She stood, having said what she came to say. "What were you expecting?"

"Well, I was going to be a charming smart-ass, and you were going to come back to church on Sunday, and then I was going to ask you out for coffee afterward."

She actually smiled. It was a nice smile.

"Stay on your own side of town, Michael," she said.

She started for the door and I let her get the last row of pews. "What did he do?"

"Cantrell?" she asked. "You name it. Drugs. Guns. Racketeering. He wants to run the entire show."

I said, "I meant God. What did he do to piss you off?"

She waited a moment and said, "Gave my mother cancer and let my father live." Then she pulled open the door.

"The door is always open here, Maggie." I called and watched it shut behind her. So much for analogies.

* * *

I got back to my office and Padi was waiting for me. "Where's Dontay?" I asked.

"Had to go home," she said. "Said he'll be back tomorrow. He wants a triple espresso mocha latte."

"That's the most expensive drink in the place," I said.

She didn't smile. She said, "Why did you want to know about the building?"

I said, "What did you find out?"

She said, "I found out that the building is owned by a company called Tri-State Holdings."

"Okay. That doesn't tell me a lot."

"It didn't tell me anything either," she said. "So I looked up who owned Tri-State Holdings."

"And?"

"Tri-State Holdings is owned by a company called TBP Incorporated."

"I'm sensing a pattern."

"It's not a pattern," she said. "It's a web." There are companies that own other companies that are owned by the first company. They have real estate all over the city, most of it in some of the worst sections of town."

"Somebody put the web together," I said.

"Somebody did." She stared at me.

I said, "And this information, was it obtained legally?"

She said, "If I tell you that, then you will know."

I said, "Is it something you could accidentally leave on the computer and I could find it when I came back from my meeting with the detective?"

She said, "Yes. That could happen. But I used the same process of websites and addresses to find this information. Somebody better than me could trace it all the way back if I leave it the way it is."

"You said no one could trace it back."

"Somebody better than me at this could," she said. "It would come back here. To you. That's why I'm asking why you want to know."

"Wouldn't they have to know that we were looking at them in order for them to come looking for us?" I asked.

"True," she said. "So you'd have to keep out of

it. You can't act on the information. And yet you've already had a visit from the police."

"They were selling tickets to a charity event." She knew I was lying.

"Are you a priest or are you Batman?" she asked.

"Dontay was into drugs," I said. "Now he wants out of drugs, but the people who sold him the drugs would prefer he keep taking them. I am relatively sure Dontay is not their sole source of income. I want to know where the drugs are coming from."

She was still looking at me in a "what are you into?" kind of way. "Let us say," she said, "that the tattoo place you asked me about is involved somehow."

"Let's say that," I repeated.

"If the people who own that building don't want you to know who they are, then we can assume that other buildings owned by the same companies who don't have owners are also involved."

"But they do have owners," I said.

"But the owners are owned by other owners who blah-blah-blah…"

"Someone is making, distributing, and selling various chemicals in the city," I said, "And if the police try to bust one, they won't be able to bust the others, because they are all owned by one another."

"Correct," she said.

"So they will constantly be after the small fish in the big pond."

"Because technically there is no big fish," she said.

"What about in the real world?"

"There's a big fish, but I can't get to it," she said. "I don't have enough information."

"You should probably go home," I said.

"What are you into here?" she asked.

"I have been told by the good protectors of the city that I am in over my head and that I should shut my mouth and let the professionals handle this. Which is what I intend to do. Whatever you did on my computer, you should undo, so that no one comes after either one of us."

She said, "Right now, no one can get to you because you've only gone so far—and as far as they could know, it's just a bunch of different corporations looking at their company profiles. If I go any further, it will create a path."

"And paths go both ways," I said.

"Right." She stood up and put on her coat. "It's supposed to snow this weekend."

"I like snow," I said.

"Have you got plans for Thanksgiving?"

"No. Are you offering?"

"My mom can't cook," she said. "I make fairly good sweet potatoes."

"I would love to come," I said.

"I'm going to invite Dontay and his grandmother too," she said. "It hasn't been more than me and Mom for a couple of years now. Thanksgiving should be about family."

"I agree." She walked around. I thought she might hug me, but it became one of those awkward kind of one-armed things that just make you feel worse.

"You can bring a date," she said.

"I'll think about it," I said. I was thinking a red-headed detective and fairly decent sweet potatoes. She left and I looked at the ceiling. HE didn't even need to say anything and I still heard his fluffy-winged little voice.

"What?" I said to the ceiling. "You said, play nice. I'm playing nice."

CHAPTER TWENTY-EIGHT

Later that night...

Micah stood on top of the building directly across from the Inkwell Tattoo Shop. He tilted his head back and felt the cold November rain fall against his skin. When the creature was "with him," rain felt different. There was no notion of just being wet. He felt every drop. He felt every nerve ending in his skin change with the temperature. He felt the rain run down his hair and drip off onto his black shirt. He felt the wet shirt cling to his gray thick skin. He didn't just stand in the rain, he became a part of it. A cold wind blew through his long black coat and the thick dense feathers in his black wings. He opened them and allowed the wind to lift him to the air.

Riding the resistance he stayed high enough to be out of the range of the street lights. "Discreet," he said to himself. The creature spoke in fewer words than Michael did. Micah had tried to understand this in the past. Eventually he had given up and accepted that things were what they were. He was Micah, not Michael. Which one was the disguise for the other? He didn't know.

Dropping lightly on the roof of the tattoo parlor, he walked slowly to the edge of the roof and placed his hands on the ledge. Tilting his head like a wolf, he listened. After hearing no sound, he pulled himself over the ledge and began to crawl down the side of the building until he reached the office where Rev. Michael Dark had confronted the man named Cantrell. He lowered his head down over the top of window. Rain had soaked his long Mohawk and the water poured off onto the sill. The office was empty. Micah thought a dramatic entrance would be in order but for whom? He pushed against the double-framed window, and the glass swung in easily. No need for locks when people are afraid of you. Micah was not afraid.

Clinging to the edge of the window's top he released the brick with his claw-like toes and allowed himself to flip right-side-up and into the office. His eyes did not need to adjust to the dark, his ears did not need to adjust to the silence.

He walked toward a gray filing cabinet. Water from his clothing and his hair puddled on the floor. The drawer made a hollow sound as it opened. It was empty. Mr. Cantrell of the King Holdings Company apparently kept his files elsewhere. He checked the other drawers without any anticipation that there might be files there.

He checked the desk. By the phone was a pad of paper. The top of the page held the words "While

you were out," and then parentheses and the words
"getting laid." A cartoon showed two people in the
act of copulation. Micah narrowed his eyes and
peered at the top page. He looked into its surface.
He found the creases of a pencil that had written a
note torn off in haste. The words said, "Graham
operation needs new distributor." Micah wondered
which of the men he had already had a discussion
with was the old distributor.

Walking around the front of the giant oak desk ,
Micah extended the nails of his right hand to their
full four inches and in one movement slashed the
modern art canvas in five rough slits.

Turning around, Micah gave serious thought to
slicing through the canvas of the reclining nude redhead. But another thought occurred to him instead.
He wondered what would happen if he hung the
portrait in Thump's office—just neatly hanging on
one of the cement pilings in amongst the 4th floor
construction of the parking garage. He could put a
note on the painting. "Good Luck In Your New
Location…" and then in big block letters
"…HELL."

Micah thought it seemed a little trite, but it
might be worth the chuckle. He lifted the portrait
off the hook behind it and nearly dropped it when
he saw the wall safe. "That," he said aloud, "was
unexpected."

He set Thump's "Good luck in your new location" present on the floor, leaning it against the
wall. Grabbing the handle on the door of the safe,
Micah turned it once…twice…he didn't expect it

would open but then again he hadn't expected to find the safe in the first place.

Placing his left hand on the wall, Micah yanked the door and broke it off the safe, taking with it a large chunk of plasterboard as well as a good bit of the concrete safe housing. Tossing the safe door on Cantrell's desk, Micah peered into the safe. Now that was really unexpected.

Sitting alone in the safe was a small piece of brightly colored plastic. A bright blue pony with big bright eyes and a purple mane. The stand on which it stood said, "My Little Pony" and "Rainbow Dash." Micah picked it up. The toy was a flash drive.

"Friendship is magic," Micah thought. He put the pony into his inner coat pocket, wondering what secrets little Rainbow Dash might hold.

The eight-foot gargoyle with the wings poking through the holes in the back of the floor length leather coat began to hum the My Little Pony theme song as looked around the room one last time, wondering if there was anything he'd missed.

Micah saw the building across the alley illuminate with the headlights of a car making the left turn. He inched quietly toward the window and looked down to see Cantrell getting out of his car, running for the blue door beneath and the sputtering exterior light. He thought about waiting where he was and seeing if he could make Cantrell wet himself when he came in. Instead, he looked again at the Mercedes parked directly beneath the win-

dow. His ear picked up the sound of expensive shoes on the stairs below.

He leaned both hands on the edge of the giant oak desk. Then bending low, he picked up the end of the desk and shoved it toward the window.

* * *

Cantrell, who had been in the business long enough to know never to rush into any room, paused without thinking as he neared the top of the stairs and heard something in his office. He reached for his gun—but even before he pulled it from the waistband of his pants, he heard the crash. He heard a dozen car alarms go off in the street. He heard people scream. Turning around, he ran back down the stairs and out the back door into the alley. His desk was standing vertically where his engine should be. The steam fumes of his obliterated radiator engulfed the alley and made him gag.

Stepping down the stairs and into the alley, he stared at two of his most expensive possessions now melded into one. He didn't even have to look to know that the bits and pieces of canvas were artwork.

A woman at the end of the alley screamed, and several men who had left the tattoo parlor looked up to see what the noise had been. One of them said, "Fuck me."

Cantrell looked up and saw something dark with large wings fly across the sky. It looked as though it had come from the top of his building and had landed on top of the bar across the street. In a moment it was gone into the rain. Cantrell stood in the rain and watched it go as his car continued to hiss loudly. No one would call 911, not in this neighborhood. He would call Thump to come and take care of the mess after he was finished. Shielding his eyes from the rain, Cantrell searched the skies for the winged creature. Deep down in the pit of his stomach, he no longer believed that this was the work of a man in a suit. This was no Batman, no Zorro. This thing was real. He was going to play this little game out to the end. When this was over, he would either own the city or be dead.

He felt surprisingly calm. He embraced this odd calmness and put his hands in his pockets and walked out of the alley. He would have whistled if he hadn't thought it might attract attention. The street was filling up now. There was nothing to tie him to the office—even the car wasn't in his name. The car was nothing. He walked out onto the wet street and entered the building again. The lights in his office still worked. The empty space where the desk had been made a glaring hole in the room. He liked that desk. Outside, people were already returning to their drinks and tattoos and other distractions. He looked at the shredded remnants of his canvas hanging on the wall.

He spotted the beautiful redhead leaning against the wall. He saw the hole where the door to his safe had been. He looked for the flash drive, knowing it would not be there. He said, "Shit." very quietly and dialed Councilman Moore's cell phone. When Moore answered, Cantrell said, "We have a problem."

CHAPTER TWENTY-NINE

In spite of the heat that the city naturally gener-
ated, the rain began to turn to snow. High above,
Micah felt the snow collect on his eyelids and skin.
He snaked out a long gray tongue and caught the
flakes before they fell through the evening smog of
the city. He flapped his wings one or two times and
lifted himself into the airstream where he rode the
current cross-cutting the city. Over Independence
Hall and the Liberty Bell building, he followed the
highway. He could actually feel the city darken
beneath him and not just in light...in life. An apart-
ment building on Graham Street made a fine land-
ing spot. He scanned the street from one end to the
other. He was looking for dim light through board-
ed windows, he was listening for the sound of quiet
voices and radios playing loud music at a soft vol-
ume. He opened his nasal cavity hunting for the
smell of a Bunsen burner. Gas. Flame. Chemicals
Voices. Sweat. Sound. Hiss. Boom. Boom Boom.
Micah took it all in. Opening himself up, he

found his way. Leaping from the building to the roof of the house next door and then the garage next to it, and finally to the pavement, he ran. The streetlights had long been destroyed by bullets fired from the windows of the bored. Micah followed all his senses until he came to a two-story house over a hundred years old. It probably could have been placed on a historical registry, had the inhabitants cared...had the historical society had anyone willing to venture into this neighborhood at any time of day. Its significance would go unnoticed and unknown.

Micah stood outside and took in the house with all his senses. He felt the hair on his back rustle. He snorted, clearing from his nostrils the profane smell of death.

He walked soundlessly to one side of the house and stood by the basement window. He heard what he guessed to be five whispered voices. There might be more who were just sitting quietly somewhere. He inhaled again and furrowed his brow, puzzling. There was an old scent in there. Sniffing, he recognized it. He wondered which of the young men inside had cancer. He wondered if the young man was aware of it. He wondered if the young man knew he'd be dead in a year if he didn't take himself out by some other means. He heard the sound of glass on glass. Someone had at least been paying attention during high school chemistry.

Walking around to the back yard he smelled the filth. Smart enough to know not to use the plumbing, the men inside had used the backyard as a toi-

let. *There were garbage bags and a rusted bed frame lying near the wooden steps leading up into the back of the house.*

He tried the doorknob. Locked. He twisted it with his hand until it broke quietly and he pushed the door open. Standing in the kitchen he could feel the heat coming up from the floor below. The counters were strewn with fast food bags and empty beer cans. There was a red Igloo cooler on the counter. In the dark, Micah could see the cool haze around it. It had been filled with fresh ice recently. Opening the top Micah was surprised to find a large stash, not of beer, but of bottled teas and cans of orange juice. "Health nuts," Micah thought.

He pulled out a brightly colored can of orange juice, and poked a whole in the top with a fingernail. He leaned against the kitchen counter, his head nearly touching the ceiling. He had folded his wings in when he entered the house. Beneath him in the basement, he heard the CD player switch to a new disk. The rap music from before was replaced by the soft painful hum of Blind Willie Johnson singing "Dark Was The Night, Cold Was The Ground." Someone groaned and made a comment about "old man music" and headed up the stairs.

As he turned the corner into the kitchen Micah caught his face in his hand, covering his mouth. The man's eyes widened, other than that, he didn't move. Micah leaned in close to the man's face as the tears began to stream down his cheeks. Micah put a fat finger to his own lips and said, "Shhhhhhhhhhh hh."

The man went into a dead faint. Micah stood there, supporting the man's weight with one hand by his cheekbones. He thought, "I should have tried that years ago," and tried not to think that Gabriel had been right.

Micah allowed the man to slip to the floor. When he took his hand away he recognized the man as one of the twelve that had visited the church.

He reached into the cooler and took another cold can of juice and began to clomp loudly down the stairs. He heard a voice say, "T-boy. Bring me one."

At the bottom of the stairs Micah could see that the next room was illuminated by a single bulb. He turned the corner and threw the can, taking out the light source. At least two of the remaining four saw him before the light went out. One of them said, "What the fuck?"

Standing in the entrance to the room, Micah's giant form was lit only by the Bunsen burners and a strong light from beneath a closet door. "Growing room," Micah thought. One of the men had turned and had seen him and tried to run. He bumped into the table, rattling the glass and falling to the floor. One of them had the good sense to open the closet door and then said, "Shit" loudly, as if he was regretting the move. A man came at Micah with a knife. Micah grabbed the man's hand and yanked him into hard concrete first. The man fell and did not get up.

Two gunshots fired. The first whizzed past Micah's ear, the second entered his upper arm above the elbow and went out the other side. Micah hissed at the burn. He walked toward the man who had pulled the trigger and grabbing his face threw him across the room to the table, full of chemicals, that shattered loudly. A Bunsen burner came disconnected from the tube, and the tube began shooting blue flame into the air.

Micah heard one set of feet running up the stairs. He heard the man trip over his sleeping co-worker on the kitchen floor. Three down. One gone. There's one more. Micah listened. Turning he saw Naws pressing himself into the corner. Naws had bandages on the side of his head. Micah saw the wires poking through the skin where the jaw had been wired back together. He was crying but couldn't open his mouth to let the sound out.

Micah walked forward as a bag of trash caught fire behind him. "Naws," Micah said, "have you been bad again?"

Naws shook his head wildly like a four-year-old caught standing by a broken vase. A bag of garbage behind Micah caught fire and began to burn quickly. Micah sighed, picked up the unconscious man at his feet, and threw him over his shoulder. Grabbing another by his shirt front. Micah walked through the flames to the stairs. He spoke quietly. "Naws, the house is on fire."

Naws began to whimper and tried to push himself further back into the corner of the room.

Micah stomped up the stairs angrily and, reaching the top, kicked the door off its hinges and threw both of his burdens out the door into the backyard.

*One of them landed on the door and made a noise,
but he didn't know which one.*

*Micah turned back and grabbed the still sleeping
T-boy from the kitchen floor and with one move
shoved him out the door onto the pile of his co-
workers.*

*Standing straight now, Micah looked at the ceil-
ing and said, "I'm going. I'm going." Like an exas-
perated parent, Micah stomped back down the
basement stairs and peered through the smoke.
Naws was still whimpering in the corner. Micah
walked through smoke, and Naws screamed as
loud as he could without moving his mouth.*

*Micah bent down into Naws' face. "Naws," he
said, "look around.* This *is your afterlife if you
don't clean up your act. Do you understand?"*

*Naws covered his face with his hands, rather
than look at the gargoyle that had just emerged
from the wall of flame. Micah sighed again and
grabbed Naws. Pulling him to his feet, he wrapped
his black coat around him and together they passed
through the flames. At the top of the stairs, the cold
wind blew in through the open door and Micah
filled his lungs with the fresh air. Naws pushed himself away and ran out the space where the door had
been. He tripped over the pile of former inhabitants
of the house, stood up, and kept running into the
wet night.*

*Micah wandered out into the yard and pulled all
of the remaining men away from the burning
house. Checking their pockets, he found five
phones between them. Turning one of the phones*

on, Micah was barely able to tap 9-1-1 on the screen with his massive fingers. A voice said, "Nine one one. What is your emergency?" Micah said quietly, "Fire," and then gently placed the phone on the ground. He put the other phones in his pocket.

He thought about going after Naws, but instead allowed the November wind to lift him into the air. He glided past the speeding fire engine as the rain pelted his face and coat. When he was high enough to hover, he checked the wound. The bullet had passed all the way through. Micah stuck his finger in the hole and pulled it out again. That would close up, he was pretty sure. It would be sore tomorrow but it would close up again.

* * *

He knew Dontay was dead before he landed. From above the church he saw his apartment balcony and knew...he just knew. Dontay had been nailed to the wood through the wrists. It was a sloppy job. Blood had poured out of the wounds and collected in a puddle on the floor of his balcony. Micah crouched saw the amount of blood and knew there was no hope. He crouched carefully on the ledge and stared at the boy's face. "I'm sorry," Micah said.

He would have to land, change, and come in through the front door if he was going to pull off discovering Dontay here. He could already see his apartment door had been broken open. He would have to find a story, make it believable, call the police and eventually sit down across from Miss Roberta and tell her that someone had nailed her grandson to a piece of wood and stuck him in the new minister's apartment. In the pit of his stomach...not his stomach...in the pit of his very soul he could feel something. It was rage. He had felt it before. He swallowed hard and pushed it down. Buried it. Covered it over. He would keep it there. Let it grow and then...soon...let it out.

CHAPTER THIRTY

A STAR OVER THE I (EYE)
A blog about nothing, written for no one in particular, by someone who pretty much stopped giving a rat's ass about things a long time ago.

ENTRY: 665.5

I can't find Dontay. I mean I don't know where he is. His grandmother called my mom and asked if he was here or if there was some event over at the church. Mom asked me. We don't know where Dontay is.

There is a big scary-looking demon thing with giant wings in his neighborhood and it doesn't like drugs and I can't find Dontay. Honestly, I'm not as scared as I think I'm supposed to be. Dontay is a good kid. Dontay is funny. Dontay said he quit doing drugs and I believe him. I'm more worried for the guys who sell the stuff. They seem to be the ones in the hospitals.

I asked Mom if she asked Dontay's grandma if she called the hospitals. Mom nodded and said, "Yes, and the police."

We both sat and worried for awhile. Then I came back in here to write.

I saw the big black scary demon thing. It was very, very big. It was loud too. You know when they interview people on television who have been through a hurricane—it's like they always have the same comment. "It sounded like a freight train." or "I could not believe how loud it was."

The big scary demon thing was ten feet high and it was turning over a car. People were screaming. Horns were blaring. It looked at me.

I know I didn't say that at our session, Dr. Conners, but it looked right at me. It told me to go home. Yes, I have been sitting on that. No, it didn't make me feel better to let it out.

Mom told me about the guy who came flying through the 7th floor window of the hospital. What do we call that? Hang glider accident? Something threw him in there. Something that doesn't like drugs but still can't seem to kill a drug dealer. I have to ask Fr. Dark what that's called. Is that grace or redemption or atonement or one of those churchy words? Maybe the demon thing just *looks* like death. Appearances can be deceiving.

I'm worried but I'm not worried. Dontay will turn up. If anything, I think the big scary demon thing is protecting him.

CHAPTER THIRTY-ONE

Red...yellow...green...blue...red...blue...orange. This was the exact order of the colored bits of glass that encircled the center of the stained glass cross that sat on my coffee table. It was completely unremarkable except for one thing. I've been in cathedrals when dawn's light shines through. I've watched lightning flash outside glass depictions of fallen angels. These little tabletop versions don't come close but you have to appreciate the effort.

I told you there was one thing that made it remarkable. I happen to know that the glass in this tabletop number came from the windshield of a car. The artist painted the glass, wrapped it in a sheet, and then beat it with a giant crescent wrench the size of a horse's leg. She then fashioned each piece together, bit by bit, until she had created the cross that now sat on my table. Miss Roberta was a wonderful woman. She had rebuilt her life the same way. Bit by bit. Now I felt like I had wrapped her life in a sheet and beat it with a wrench.

I was sitting on my couch as a variety of cops and other law enforcement types wandered my over-large apartment. Several men in red jackets had removed Dontay's body. They took dozens of pictures. They put the body in a black bag and strapped it to a stretcher. I knew all this was happening behind me as I sat and stared at Miss Roberta's cross.

They kept sneaking looks at me. The priest sitting on his couch in the middle of a crime scene. I could almost hear their thoughts. They were thinking the same thing a lot of other people think when they see priests these days. They thought I might be some kind of monster. Now, that would be ironic.

Lucas Haberkorn sat to my left. He had a clear view of the balcony but was not looking. He was looking at me and saying nothing. Thank God, he was saying nothing. He's sat with many people in their worst moments. He's held the hand of the dying. He's wise enough now to understand words are meaningless...presence is everything.

Back in my day we called this sitting shiva. You came. You sat. You kept your mouth shut. That was how we grieved back then.

Detective Maggie Grafton came over to us. She had been asleep not too long ago. I wonder what that phone call was like. She was wearing her long brown trench coat over what I assumed was yesterday's shirt and jeans. She had combed her short red hair with her fingers and was wearing glasses instead of contacts. Is it wrong of me to say how beautiful she was? Probably. Something about powerful women gets to me. She touched Haberkorn on the shoulder and said, "Father, may we have a moment, please?"

Haberkorn nodded and stood. "Michael, can I get you something?" He had managed to get into a Temple University sweatshirt and pants, but I noticed he had forgotten his socks. I waved him off, and he wandered out into the hall as Detective Maggie took his seat.

I asked, "Are you going to say, 'I told you so'?"

She looked at the cross too. "Would that make anything better?"

I said, "No."

She said, "Then, no." She sighed deeply. "You weren't in the building when this happened?"

"I was getting a cheese steak," I lied.

"At two in the morning?"

"Haberkorn said that's when you find the most interesting atmosphere."

"Can they verify that?" she asked. "That you were there?"

"Probably," I said. "Was crowded but they could probably confirm it."

She said, "Well, the camera you have downstairs hasn't worked since 1988."

"Budget cuts," I told her.

"There's a boot print on the door downstairs and one on your apartment door. Same shoe, looks like. Bigger than yours."

I looked over at her. "They think I did this. They think I crucified a kid in my own home."

"They think everything," she said.

We sat there and listened to the ambient noise of an apartment where something horrific has taken place.

"We've had similar things happen," she said. "Long before you got here, so we're thinking it's a pattern. We had a car dealer whose son got in heavy with a dealer and someone ran him over in the showroom. Had a bartender whose little brother was force-fed alcohol till his heart stopped."

I nodded.

"This was a message, Reverend. This was someone telling you to get out of their business."

"I had one talk with him."

"That's it?" she said. "You didn't go back after I told you to drop it?"

"No." I really wanted to grab the stained glass cross and heave it across the room.

"You didn't go to his office tonight and shove his desk out the window?"

I gave her my absolute best what-the-hell-are-you-talking-about expression. "I've been here all night. I got hungry. I went for a cheese steak."

She said, "You didn't visit a drug lab on Graham Street?"

"I don' know where Graham Street is," I said. "I haven't lived here a month."

A cop in a blue uniform behind me said, "Welcome to the City of Brotherly Love."

"Sergeant," Grafton said, and the cop moved away to do other cop things.

I leaned forward and picked up the glass cross on the table. "I saw a movie once about a vampire.

This young kid goes after a vampire and he's got a cross, like that's going to help him. The vampire shows up and says, 'That's only as powerful as the faith you put in it.' Then the vampire bites his neck."

"I'm a Bela Lugosi fan myself," she said. "Him and Boris Karloff are the only monsters I need."

I half-smiled. "Don't forget Lon Chaney, Jr."

"Wolf-man," she said.

"Zombies?"

"Not a big zombie fan. *The Night of the Living Dead* gave me nightmares."

"Dontay liked zombies," I said, putting the cross back. "I was showing him Bible verses where the dead come back to life and walk around."

Grafton said, "Reverend, in a few minutes a man with long black hair and thick black-framed glasses is going to come through your door. His name is Perkins. He's going to have a camera and will probably take a few hundred pictures of everything in your apartment. Then two guys in coveralls will come and take the body down to the street. You probably shouldn't be here for that."

"Has someone told his grandmother?"

"A few minutes ago," she said, "an older woman came into the police station worried about a missing grandson. He fit the description."

"Someone take her home?"

"She's at the morgue," Grafton said. "She wanted to see him."

"Can you take me there?"

"Sure," she said. "Do you have somewhere else you can stay tonight?"

"Got a couch in my office."

"It might be a few days."

"This part of the building used to be dorm rooms. This apartment used to be two. They took out the ceiling and made it one. They bricked up the windows. There's a smaller balcony above mine. No window."

"This is three times the size of my apartment. What do they soak you for rent?"

"Comes with the job."

"Nice."

"Yeah," I said, "but then you literally live at your job. There's no place to go when..." I saw a light shine through the stained glass cross and project an image on the good detective. She didn't seem to notice. I looked over and saw Gabriel hovering outside my balcony. No one else did. He was looking at the body in the bag. I was lost in thought and realized I hadn't finished what I was saying. I looked at Grafton wondering where I had left off.

"There was nothing you could have done," Grafton said. "Someone was watching your place. Waiting for you to leave."

I stood up and so did she. "Let me tell my boss that I'm leaving. He may come with us."

She nodded.

The colored light dimmed, and I looked back out the glass door to the balcony. The angel had gone.

CHAPTER THIRTY-TWO

A STAR OVER THE I (EYE)
A blog about nothing, written for no one in particular,
by someone who pretty much stopped giving a rat's
ass about things a long time ago.

ENTRY: 667

Okay, I used to have this friend named Kristen. She used to take stuff apart. Speak-n-Spell, Mom's alarm clock, she leveled Barbie's "Dream Dune Buggy" in an hour. She wasn't trying to be destructive, and she never really got good at putting things back together. She would lay out a sheet on her floor and line up all the pieces. She just liked looking at things that way. Eventually her mother got tired of it and started buying Kristen blenders and vacuum cleaners and other small gadgets at garage sales. Didn't matter if they worked or not. She'd give them to her daughter and Kristen would have it in pieces...all lined up on the floor of her bedroom.

This is my life.

It's like I have all the parts, they're just lined up neat and orderly on a sheet, and I have no idea how they go together. Mom said she got an email from the church. She told me about Dontay. I said I wanted to go talk to Dontay's grandmother but Mom seems to think I would be a bother. I told her I wanted to go and talk to Fr. Dark and she said no I wasn't going into that neighborhood when it was dark.

She said I could go to the funeral.

How's that for a sentence?

She said I could go to the funeral.

I read once that Hemingway got into some kind of contest with other writers to see who could write a story in the fewest words. That's my entry.

She said I could go to the funeral.

I'll take my prize now. Can you please make Dontay not dead any more?

No?

Then fuck you.

I'm looking at all these pieces of my life. Why don't they go together? Why did this happen? I really have this strong desire to blame Fr. Dark but it's not his fault. Did you catch that, Dr. Conners? I'm not blaming anybody except the people who murdered Dontay. They have responsibility. But would they have done what they did if the big scary demon thing hadn't shown up? Would they have done what they did if Fr. Dark hadn't stuck his nose into something it wasn't supposed to be stuck in? He was trying to make them lay off Dontay and instead they killed him. The drugs would have done it eventually but Dontay was cleaning up his act.

Stupid pieces.
Stupid life.
Stupid scary demon thing.
Stupid Fr. Dark
Stupid mom.
Stupid Dr. Conners (yeah, I know you didn't have anything to do with it but you made me write this stupid blog so you're stupid too.)
Stupid church.
Stupid God.
Stupid.
Stupid.
Stupid.
Fuck.
Fuck.
Fuck.

CHAPTER THIRTY-THREE

Bullshit.

You know those cheap novels and the bad movies on Lifetime where the bad guys actually show up to the funeral of the person they murdered and then sit at a distance and only the hero seems to know? That's bullshit. You know how ministers are supposed to have all the right things to say in times of great tragedy and be of great comfort to all those around? That's bullshit too. I know Dontay was in a better place. I've been there. I have heard the voice of God. I have felt his breath on my skin. I have looked into the face of Jesus (he has his mom's eyes). I know all these things, and yet they don't make one damn bit of difference when I look at the face of Dontay's grandmother.

How she must hate me.

Detective Maggie Grafton showed up to the funeral. Kind of her. Rev. Haberkorn led the serv-ice. He saw my incompetence as grief, and pretty much did the whole thing himself. He let me silently assist him. I looked for Thump. I honestly did. I thought maybe he might show or send his ecumenical goon squad. Bad guys are smart. This is not a movie.

Detective Maggie shook Dontay's grandmother's gloved hand. I did not hear what she said. I know his grandmother leaned in real close and whispered something in the detective's ear. I imagined it was something thoughtful and kind, with just a twinge of "blow the bastard away for me." At least that's what I imagined it was. It made me feel better when Maggie nodded and patted her hand.

I doubted she would. She would arrest him and put him away along with all the others she had been putting away for years only to see them back on the street again. She would not kill the man for the satisfaction of doing so. I, on the other hand, had so such problem. If Thump or Cantrell had shown up at the funeral (even at a distance), I would have changed into my "working clothes" right there in front of God and everyone and ripped his heart out through his chest and then replaced it through his mouth.

Padi was a statue through the service. She wore a black dress and a black veiled hat that looked like she was playing dress-up with her grandmother's clothes. She also wore two dark black crosses, one hanging from each ear. If anyone had had the stones to tell her she was dressed inappropriately they would have had to look at her face, they would have seen her eyes, and they would have kept their damn mouth shut.

After the funeral she hugged me, very hard. I felt just a moment of a shudder in her and I thought she might break down but she didn't. I kissed the top of her head, just beside the hat and whispered, "Meet me in my office later." She looked up and nodded and then went off to hug Dontay's grandma.

Haberkorn said, "Nice job" to me.

I said, "I didn't do anything."

"How hard was it to keep it together?"

"Hardest thing I've ever done."

"Nice job," he repeated.

It was kind of him, but I didn't feel like I was doing my job very well.

Gabriel was there. I didn't see him right away but I knew he was there. I could smell him. I knew he wanted to talk. Haberkorn and I walked Dontay's grandmother back to the limo. She was clutching the jacket he had been wearing the first time I met him.

I told her again how sorry I was. She put a gloved hand on my face. She said, "Wasn't your fault child. He was so happy these last few days. Acted like he was his own man. Hadn't seen that in him in a long time. You put that there."

How could I tell her that I may as well have been the one to put him put him on a piece of wood on my balcony? How to you say that to a person.

It took twenty minutes for them to fill in the grave after everyone else had gone. The filling in was done by three cemetery workers who had slightly more combined IQ points than they did teeth. I stood there in my robe and watched them.

Rev. Haberkorn had left me to drive myself back to the church where the Ladies Circle had prepare a reception of tiny sandwiches and flavorless cookies. I wanted a coffee.

I waited for Larry, Moe, and Curly to leave, and then I stood by the grave and I waited.

He didn't do one of his fancy entrances and I give him credit for not starting out the conversation with, "I told you so." He was simply there and waited awhile before we talked. I looked at him. He was floating there. An icy wind blew and cut me down to my bones. I saw his feathers ruffle. If he felt the breeze or the cold he didn't show it. I was sure he didn't. He never let himself feel anything. I saw he was hovering six inches off the ground again and it really pissed me off. His robe was immaculate and mine was wet with dew and snow.

"Don't do what you are thinking of doing," he said finally and flatly.

"What happens if I do?" I asked.

"This assignment has no end date," he said. "I can leave you right here. You may like it, but you've seen what comes next. I can just let you live out you human days all over again and you can keep playing priest and breathing smog and burying children, and watching your friends die. You can feel your bones get old and your body wear out and every day you get to experience the disconnection from the Creator more profoundly than anyone else because you've been there. You want to play dress-up, fine, but don't do what you're thinking about doing."

There it was. It was the basic source of so many of our disagreements over the years. He thought leaving me here was punishment. "You've got dirt on your robe," I said.

"No, I don't." He didn't even look down.

"I know," I said. "You never have dirt on your robe. Why is that?"

"This is not helping," he said. "You still have a job."

I scraped a handful of snow off a headstone. I doubted the owner would mind. I started to form a snowball with my hands. "You can take this job and shove it."

"Micah," he said.

"That's a country song, Gabriel." I told him. He started to speak but I interrupted him. "Country music. It's sad and its happy and it's about the pain of losing and the honor of standing tall. Have you ever heard country music? I mean the really sad stoned-at-the-jukebox stuff?"

"You were told not to..." He was ignoring me and it just made me angrier.

"You don't know anything about country music. You sit up there and you dance around singing praises and you think everybody should be like you. They can't, Gabriel. You want to know why? Because you're not human. You never were. You come down here and you don't let anything touch you. You don't let anything get near you. You don't see, touch or taste anything."

I threw the snowball as hard as I could and it splattered against the face of an angel statue that stood over the grave of someone who had died in 1959. The statue's face had been worn down, but the body language seemed to suggest it was waiting for the occupant of the grave to wake up.

"That's you," I said. "That stone angel. That's you."

I didn't even see him move. All I know was that I was suddenly off my feet and we were flying across the cemetery until I slammed into a tree six feet off the ground. He had dropped his clipboard and had me by the front of my robe. I didn't even try to struggle. He could have broken me in half if he wanted to. I looked into his white eyes and I saw fury.

"And what are you, Micah?" he said into my face. "What are you but one of those stone gargoyles that sits out on that balcony. Hanging around scaring people but other than that not accomplishing much until you fall off the wall and get someone killed." I started to struggle under his grasp but he was having none of it. "Do you want to know why? Do you want to know why I don't touch the ground or get my wings dirty or sit with you and have a cheese steak? Do you want to know why, Micah?"

I waited.

"Because that's my gift," he said. "That's the gift I was given in return for being the servant who gets to take a flaming sword to a city. That's the gift I get for being the one who got to fly down and collect all those babies when Herod decided to go on a spree. I got to feel nothing when His children, his *chosen* children were lined up and gassed until their eyes bulged out of their heads and their tongues turned blue. I got to feel nothing. That was my gift."

He shook me hard and I banged the back of my head against the tree. "You get to feel everything. Then you complain when it hurts." With that he dropped me, and I fell to the ground in a heap. I looked up at him and he spread his wings out. It was still impressive, no matter how many times I make fun of him and tell him that mine are better. The sight was still impressive. He said, "Don't do what you're thinking about doing."

Okay, this part is going to sound trite but you know that old cartoon about the green grouchy guy who steals Christmas? Sure you do. Who doesn't? Remember the scene where the little girl who is "no more than two" catches the Grinch in the act of shoving the tree up? In the story it says "he heard a small sound like the coo of a dove."

It was just a plaintive little "ah." sound. We both heard it. Me and Gabriel. Me sitting on the wet ground and him hovering above me in all his winged magnificence. We both looked and saw Padi. She was standing by a tree. The veil was lifted off her eyes and she was staring.

She didn't run. I'll give her that. She didn't scream.

Here's the thing. Humans aren't supposed to see angels, so of the three of us I think Gabriel may have been the most surprised.

He was gone in an instant. There was no way she

should have seen him. It doesn't happen. Not without permission. I could tell by the look on Gabriel's face in that instant that the permission had not come from him and technically there aren't that many higher-ups in this game. I stood up and looked at Padi. "I told you I'd meet you later in my office."

She blinked three times and said, "That...that..."

"My office," I said. I put a finality on it. It was a tone I hadn't used in years. It was the tone that said, "Give me all your money or I will kill you right now and rape your wife."

Padi turned and left.

How was I going to explain this one?

* * *

I pulled into the church parking lot and walked over to Java Joe's. I didn't know if Padi was hanging out in my office or not but I ordered two coffees and sat down at the counter. As Dwight poured my coffee, I looked at my hands and wrists. I pushed my thumb against my wrist, between the two bones, and tried to imagine a nail there. If a crucifixion is done properly, there is surprisingly little blood loss. Death comes from suffocation not from bleeding. Dontay's was not done properly. Dontay bled out his life. Thump, not being a centurion of the Roman empire, had not known what he was doing.

Dwight brought the coffees over with a bag with two of his large blueberry muffins. "Are these for you and the young lady? The friend of Dontay's?"

I nodded and took out my wallet. He waved me off. "Not today," he said. He spoke the words out loud. Despite his hearing loss he wanted to say the words, to pay his respects. I appreciated that. His speech was nearly perfect despite his hearing loss. "Father I want you to know how sorry I am. People are hoping the police will do something about it this time."

I looked at him. He could see by the look on my face I was debating with myself over whether or not I should say what I was thinking.

"What?" He said it and signed it at the same time.

"Dwight," I said, "I want to do something about it myself."

He waited. There were two other people in the shop, so I silently signed my question. "Do you still have any access to explosives?"

CHAPTER THIRTY-FOUR

I edged the door of my office open with my foot and saw the vast collection of M&M's scattered across my floor. The ceramic bowl they had been sitting in was shattered and lying in various places around the room. I still had my blanket and pillow on the couch.

Padi was actually sitting in the guest chair opposite my desk. She didn't look up when I came in. "I owe you a new bowl," she said.

"Was here when I got the office," I said. "Was only a few weeks ago"

"Seems like longer," she said.

"That it does." I carefully stepped around the brightly colored land mines and crushed only a few of them into the carpet. I sat down in my own chair, handed her a coffee, and put the muffins in the center of the desk.

"The M&Ms. They said something mean?"

"They looked happy," she said. "I wasn't in the mood for happy."

"Duly noted," I said. "Someday I'll be sure and warn your future boyfriend."

"He'll have to take me as I am," she said.

"And learn to duck."

She almost smiled at that one.

Then the silence came. I sighed. "I'm guessing you have some questions."

"Only about a million."

"Is there one you'd like to start with?"

She opened her mouth, then hesitated. She opened it again and then stopped. I thought for a second she might cry but she physically swallowed it back.

I said, "How about if I ask the first question. You answer and then it will be your turn. Okay?"

She nodded.

"What's your favorite color of M&M?"

"Green. But not the horny green. The green they come out with at Christmas time. What's yours?"

"Yellow," I said. "What about Lifesavers? Favorite flavor?"

"Peppermint. Yours?"

"Butterscotch. How old were you when you had your first cup of coffee?"

"Was that an angel kicking your ass?"

Okay, now we were off to the races. "First," I clarified, "he wasn't kicking my ass but yes, that was an angel."

"He was kicking your ass."

"Agree to disagree."

"You know an angel. That was a real angel. As in multitude of heavenly host."

"That was the angel Gabriel," I told her. "God's messenger."

"You know an angel." It wasn't a question. Her eyes widened a little and she said, "Do you know the big scary demon thing too?"

I nodded. "Not a demon. Another angel. They don't all wear white."

"So it's all real."

"What is?"

"God. Jesus. Angels. Mary. All of it."

"It's all real."

"And heaven is too."

"Heaven too."

"And Dontay is there."

"Oh, yes."

"So are you like a minister to the undead?"

"Well, I was thinking of opening a shelter for homeless souls."

"Don't they all go to heaven?"

"Some get lost."

She sat for a moment, her eyes darting back and forth as if she were scanning a screen for her next question.

"Is it easier when you have all the answers ahead of time?" she asked.

"I don't know what you mean."

"Somebody dies. They call in the minister. The minister sits and offers all the right words and people feel less shitty. Then they feel a little less shitty everyday until they don't feel shitty anymore. I just want to know if that's easier when you're the one with the answers?"

"I've had a shitty day too," I said.

"I'm sorry. I know it's been hard..."

"Don't worry about it," I said. "I knew what you meant. But to answer your question...a little...but not much."

"Do all ministers see angels and get their asses kicked?"

"He didn't kick my ass, and no. Not all ministers see angels. Very, very few do. Which makes their faith all that more amazing."

She leaned across my own desk and looked at me. "Why didn't the big scary angel save Dontay?"

I sipped my coffee. "He was breaking up a crack house on the other side of town."

She shook her head like her hair was full of ants. It was too much information to take in all at once.

We both sat there in silence for awhile. Neither one of us eating.

Finally I said, "Padi. I'm going to ask you something that could come at a great personal risk, but I trust you. Do you trust me?"

"Implicitly," she said, and I suddenly thought of the Word-A-Day calendar in the little diner with good pancakes.

"Do you remember when you once asked me if I was into something and I told you that I wasn't?"

She nodded.

"I sort of am," I said. "I think I know who did this to Dontay and I'm not feeling the need to let the police handle it. I think there are too many people who could simply walk away and never see the consequences."

She waited a moment before nodding this time.

I took a deep breath. "What you accomplished on my computer before. Could you do more?"

"Not without more information, and not without a greater risk of them tracing it back to you."

"I'm not worried about that part," I said. "I am worried that they may, in some way, trace it back to you."

"I don't work here," she said. "I'm just your student. I only come in for the coffee."

I reached into my desk drawer and took out the four iPhones that I had collected from various individuals I had met over the last few days.

"What are those?"

I said, "We recently had a donation to our program that provides phones to women in abusive relationships. They just showed up here. Just by themselves. And I was wondering if there might be information on them that could link certain people to certain places and activities."

She nodded. She knew she was wading in deep.

I hesitated, "I have one other thing that could be useful," I said. "However I have no reason for having it. It wasn't a...uh...donation. If I give it to you there is every reason to believe that the people who killed Dontay will have a problem with me learning new information."

"I'm not following," she said.

I reached into the breast pocket of my black jacket and pulled out the plastic pony.

For just a second she was a six-year-old girl. "I love *My Little Pony!*"

I turned it so she could see it was a flash drive. "I could learn things off of this, too," I said. "But I think it's encrypted, and I need someone who can give me the information and hide *if* I have to tell them to hide."

She looked at me. "And you don't want to give this information to the police, because..."

"...because I don't," I said.

"Are you going to send an angel to dismember the people who murdered Dontay?"

"If only," I thought. What I said was, "I think there are others who can do more than the police can at this point." I set the flash drive in the center of my desk and she stared at it.

"You can leave now," I said. "You can get up and walk out and we'll pretend this conversation never happened, or I can go get a broom and dustpan to clean up the mess. That could take me a few hours—I hear the broom closet is on the other side of the building."

She didn't move.

"I'll be right back with a broom," I said. I stood up and retraced my steps through the M&M mine field.

CHAPTER THIRTY-FIVE

There's an old Monty Python album where you can find a skit about a place called "Happy Valley." It's a place where everyone is happy all the time and no one is sad or grumbly. And the reason, according to John Cleese's narration, "is that all the sad and grumbly people had been put to death the year before."

Councilman Chris Moore's office worked that way. He was a real estate developer and member of the city council. He had run against Councilwoman Harriet Bartow in the last race, and won. She had been the incumbent. When he questioned her business practices, she did not flinch. When he questioned her sexuality, she produced a boyfriend. When she wiped the floor with him in one public debate, people said the election was over. Chris Moore knew it wasn't over until he said it was over.

He was wired into the world, and when he could find no legitimate dirt on his opponent he found a dealer who was willing to admit to selling cocaine to Ms. Bartow when she was in college. The dealer speculated that this drug use might have been the reason for her miscarriage. But of course he didn't have any medical records to back that up—because he was lying through his teeth.

The dealer's name was Jude Cantrell and after his testimony he joined real estate developer Chris Moore's program to get young men off the streets and into proper business and college programs to help create a better Philadelphia.

Only happy people worked for Councilman Moore. Only happy *loyal* people. Most were legitimately happy. Councilman Moore was kind, remembered everyone's birthday, and gave fat Christmas bonuses. Many of the employees from his real estate company moved over to his Councilman's office. He had a small office in City Hall, but he preferred to do most of his work from his office in the Penner Building downtown. He leased four offices on the 65th floor. He could see the entire city.

He had spent the day alone in his office, pondering what to do about the Cantrell situation. In a way he liked Cantrell and had hopes for him. Up until recently, things had seemed to be going well. He knew what Cantrell was into and took his cut. He knew when Cantrell tried to hold back some of the money that was owed, but he let it go. He knew how many labs were on the South Side and had full trust that any possible information that might link the labs to Cantrell could never reach his desk. Cantrell knew better than that.

Now Cantrell was dealing with a new situation. Moore had been asked several times about the flying gargoyle. At first he joked and said it sounded like a beverage from his "drinking days." Moore had a chit from AA that he had stolen from a college roommate. He didn't drink publicly . If someone mentioned it he simply held up the chit (clipped to his key chain) and pretended to get a lump in his throat.

People would applaud and stop asking about it.

Flying gargoyle or monster or Batman, Moore didn't care. He didn't want to hear about it from Cantrell anymore. He wanted the situation dealt with, so they could start buying property next year and start developing the year after that. The Penner Building was the tallest building in the city. Moore had already sketched out the design for a building ten floors higher. Right in the middle of South Side. The people would praise him for cleaning up the neighborhoods. Businesses would move in. The property values that he had driven down would go back up again and he would sell them one lot at a time. It would be a new yuppies' paradise.

He sat chewing on his pencil when his cell phone beeped. The screen said, "You have 1 message."

Moore hated the little screen messages. He detested people who used them and wrote cute little slogans that shortened words to numbers: "ME 2" and "BRB." Most of all, he hated when people made faces out of punctuation. A secretary had said they were called emoticons. She had begun using them on her inter-company emails to him. A few days later, a security guard happened to find some company-sensitive software in her car and she was fired. Moore hated emoticons.

The screen on his expensive phone read, "Look out your window, asswipe. ;)"

CHAPTER THIRTY-SIX

Elmer Peterson had been in trouble since the day he started school. He came home from his first day in kindergarten with a note pinned to his shirt that his mother read, then promptly backhanded him in the mouth.

When Elmer was seventeen he had earned a permanent desk in the in-school suspension room. Elmer was fairly good at getting close to the expulsion line without crossing it. Fighting. Cigarettes. Stealing. These things bought him three weeks in a cubicle in ISS. Drugs. Alcohol. Threatening a teacher. Sexual Harassment. These things bought him three weeks of expulsion. Elmer needed to get through his senior year. All he had to do was stay out of trouble.

In the cubicle next to his a chess-club nerd had finished all his work for the day. Tony, the young man in question, had received three weeks of ISS for hacking into the school's computer system. Apparently, a cheerleader had offered him a glimpse of her boobs in return for a B in chemistry. Tony got caught and readily named the young lady in question who denied everything and broke into tears in the vice-principals office (actually, she had made a similar deal with the vice-principal; they were married six months after her graduation and divorced a year later).

Elmer saw Tony working a new map for his Dungeons and Dragons club meeting. One character sketch bore a striking resemblance to Elmer himself. After Tony's head and been shoved into the desk top and his glasses bitten in half, he confessed that the word "settico" (written beneath the sketch) was from an Italian word that meant a knife with two edges, one straight and one serrated. Elmer liked the word and adopted it as his official nickname. Settico. It didn't occur to him that Tony might be lying to him. The kid looked Italian enough so he probably knew these things. Elmer was now Settico, the knife with two edges (settico in Italian is where the English language gets the word "septic" as in "Oh, my God, the septic tank overflowed").

Seven years later Settico stood in the first floor of a building that had been, among other things, a donut shop, a hot dog shop, a flower shop, and a pedicure boutique. Currently they manufactured crystal meth. Settico didn't understand how the process worked, but—as with everything else he was fairly competent at—he simply copied exactly what he had been shown, with no variation or additions of his own. If he did this, he made money.

If he chose to screw around with the recipe, Thump beat the hell out of him. Settico chose the former.

Settico knew that Thump worked for Cantrell. He imagined that Cantrell worked for somebody else, but that wasn't his business. What you didn't know, you couldn't testify to in a court of law. Then again, if you spilled everything you might be able to cut a deal and get probation. Then again, if you got probation you'd have to leave the city because everybody you spilled on would come and try and kill you. Then again if they were in prison they couldn't very well come after you. These were the things that Settico thought about.

His cell phone made a deet-deet-deet sound and he pulled it out of his pocket. The screen read, "Settico means 'shit'."

"What the fu…" Settico started to say—then his phone deet-ed again and this time the screen read, "Your building will begin burning to the ground in 15 seconds."

It would have been a bit of irony if Settico had simply said "Shit" at this point. Instead he said "Mother," and turned to his friends. "I think we need to leave."

His co-workers all looked at him and he said. "I just got a text that says our building will catch on fire in 15 seconds." The seven of them looked at each other for the remaining 7 seconds that had not been taken up by Settico's explanation. Then they heard the sound on the roof that made them think the text message was correct, and they bolted from the building and were gone from the scene before the first fire truck arrived.

CHAPTER THIRTY-SEVEN

Dwight felt that he had truly outdone himself.

He had been worried when the new priest had spoken to him about explosives, but once he learned the plan (or at least the parts that the priest was willing to share) he was much more receptive. He loved his city, and apart from two years in the first Gulf War and eight months in a rehabilitation center in DC, he had never lived anywhere else. He had never wanted to. Now he lay awake in his bed, staring at the ceiling, waiting to see the red flashing light reflected on plaster above him. He liked the fire engines most. The horns were so loud that he could feel the vibrations on his skin and in his ears, and sometimes it was like he was actually hearing again.

Father Dark had requested a bomb that would make an incredibly loud noise and produce a tremendous amount of smoke but do very little actual damage to a building and to surrounding buildings.

Using five-gallon drums, a collection of bed-sheets from the local second-hand store, and some household chemicals, Dwight created a very loud very smoky firecracker—enough to scare the individual inside and to bring the police and fire departments to the scene almost instantly.

He wanted to ask the good Reverend how he intended to install these devices on the roofs of the homes and buildings in question, but he didn't. He just lay awake in his bed. When the flashing red light flitted across the ceiling, followed by three more in rapid succession, Dwight rolled over and slept better than he had in years.

CHAPTER THIRTY-EIGHT

Councilman Moore stood at his window and watched as three of the buildings within his range of vision seemed to burst into flame simultaneously. He didn't need to ask what buildings they were. He didn't need to ask whether the buildings on the southeast side of town were experiencing similar difficulties.

He went to the phone on his desk and jabbed the intercom to Tony's office so hard he nearly pushed his finger through the machine. He heard the beep on the other end. He waited. When no one picked up, Moore replaced the receiver, disconnected the cord from the back of the phone, and flung it across the room where it shattered against the wall near the doorway just as Tony Robertson, who had been on the receiving end of various pieces of flung office equipment, barely flinched as the debris rattled on the floor.

"Bad day?"

Moore said, "I was just trying to reach you."

"I'm already here."

Moore tossed the cell phone to him. Tony looked at the screen and smiled. "You think that's funny?" Moore shouted.

"What's funny," said Tony, "is that the same message has come over just about every computer in the office."

Moore stepped back. He inhaled deeply and said "Fuck" under his breath. He calmly turned back to his own private hacker and said, "Dump everything."

"What?"

"Dump everything. Whatever fail-safe system you set up. Dump it all. Make it look like an accident. Lose all the property files. Lose everything. Make it all go away. Nothing is traceable back to this office. Make all our files, everything on Cantrell and his distributors vanish. Dump it all. I want it gone immediately. You can do this?"

Robertson nodded. He had a fail-safe in place. It would all be gone.

"Then," the councilman said, "can you tell me where that message came from?"

Robertson smirked. "I can give you that in a minute."

"Not to me," Moore said. "Call Cantrell. Tell him to make whoever sent that message go away."

Tony nodded and stepped on the pieces of the desk phone as he left the room.

Councilman Chris Moore went back to his window and watched his properties burn. He watched the fire trucks weave through the traffic. He thought about every cent he was going to lose in the next three minutes.

He mentally began to write his speech expressing condolences to the families of the people who lost their lives in the fires. He thought that maybe, just maybe, he could get his man at the *Enquirer* to bury the story about the real estate magnate who had a system-wide shutdown on the night of the fire and had permanently lost countless files and how long they expected it would take before the company was up and running again. He went to his desk and began to jot these thoughts down on paper.

He also thought about what it would feel like to jab his thumbs into Cantrell's eye sockets, but he didn't write those thoughts down.

CHAPTER THIRTY-NINE

Thump stood in his office—the roof of the parking garage. He could hear the sirens all over the city. He could smell the smoke, depending on which way the wind was blowing. His cell phone had been ringing non-stop for the last half-hour, all of the calls from half-crazed dealers who all said that their cells had gone off and warned them to get out just before the shit hit the fan.

Thump looked off into the city toward the church. Whatever that thing was, it didn't like to kill. To Thump, that had been the ultimate feeling of power. Death or life in his hand. Take away all someone has or give it all back. That's power. How could you be as big and as mean as that thing and not be able to kill? Thump assumed it had something to do with the priest. Maybe the priest was controlling it. Maybe the priest had connections in places other than heaven. Darker, warmer places.

Thump had tried to imagine what the priest had done when he walked into his apartment. It was amazing how easy it was to get into the building. When he had yanked the first security camera off the wall and found it was full of dust, he knew there would be no problem. He dragged the wood up the stairs and then went back for Dontay's body. He decided the cross idea was a stroke of genius. Very creative. Most people would probably think the priest had done it. Wouldn't be a surprise to some people. They'd see it on the news and they'd say, "Yeah, that's what they're all like." Mostly Thump had nailed the boy to the cross to piss off the gargoyle. He had seen the gargoyles on the side of the building when he had broken into the priest's apartment. That thing was a gargoyle, Thump decided. That was another thing that was going to make him a better manager than Cantrell. Thump could take things as they were. Thump decided that killing the boy first before he nailed him up was proof that he had a streak of mercy in him. Mercy was good. It would serve him well when he took over Cantrell's job.

His phone beeped again and Thump saw it was Cantrell's number. He assumed Cantrell was up to his ass in it by now. This was his moment, and Thump was going to enjoy it.

He hit the talk button. "Hey, Asshole."

There was just a moment of silence on the other end, and then, "Thump?"

Thump laughed.

"You calling *me* an asshole?"

"That's right, Asshole." Thump said. "Looks

like tonight is your going-out-of-business sale. It going to be a fire sale?" Thump laughed again.

Thump could hear Cantrell trying to keep it together. "You remember that kid you killed. You remember him? Well somebody else in that building is the one who set the labs on fire. That fucking priest is sending messages. He's still in his fucking building. Now all the shit is coming down and you and me are standing in the middle of it all because you had to go and get creative. Now get your fucking ass over there and finish the job and get his computer or we're all dead. You fuckin' hear me, *asshole*?"

Thump took a deep breath. He had won. First one to lose his cool is the loser. Thump could hear Cantrell shake. "Do it yourself," Thump said calmly.

"You want to fuckin' say that again." Cantrell was raging now.

"I said do it yourself. I'm turning in my resignation. You're the one who's got his name on things. Me, I'm just the hired help but I'm taking over as of tomorrow. When the smoke clears, who do you think my man in the glass building is going to want to rebuild?"

"You're a dead man," Cantrell said.

"Yeah?" said Thump. "Who you think you're going to get to come after me? All your people are running for their lives or been beat to shit."

"I'm going to do it myself," Cantrell said. "I'm going to go kill that fucking priest and then I'm going to find you and I'm going to cut your balls off and shovel them down your throat."

Thump regretted his next words. "*Bon appetit.*" He hung up the phone and immediately thought of a dozen better things to say. He would have owned that whole conversation, had it not been for that last comeback. Thump wondered if there was a book on How To Be Funny or Snappy Comebacks. He'd look it up later.

For now, he was willing to wait. He had pissed off something much bigger than Cantrell, and whatever it was, it seemed like it was taking charge of this particular night. Thump would not allow that. Tonight was his night. He decided if the thing wanted to fight, it would come to him. He walked down to the floor below to the construction shed to get what he was going to need.

CHAPTER FORTY

Smoke always makes me think about things I don't like to think about. My father was a blacksmith. He worked metals. Even when he didn't have a fire burning in his shop, the smell was always in his clothes and his hair. I remember hugging him as a kid and smelling the smoke. It was just the way he smelled.

This smoke wasn't pure like that smoke. This smoke was burning more than wood. It was chemicals and roofing tar. It was garbage. There was a place near where I grew up that burned garbage. We didn't have landfills and such. Everyone took their trash over to this place called Gehenna. That was where you burned your trash. Dogs ran free in the fires there, eating what they could pull out of the flames. Those of us who learned to hang between the piles of burning trash, we usually ate cooked dog.

I was a kid when I took my first *human* life. It was a guy I had known since I was small. His name was Judah. He had money that was mine. We had both pushed the tax collector off his horse. We grabbed his wife (women always carried the money in those days), we took the money, and we ran. Later Judah gave me about a third of the money and he looked to me like he was just daring me to say something, 'cause we were friends. I told him to give me my share or I'd kill him. He laughed at me. I drew my sword and I ran him through.

I just remember he looked so surprised.

He fell against me. I took the money and I left his body where it was. I figured it would either burn or the dogs would eat it.

After that, I didn't matter. Nothing mattered. I took money. Those that didn't give it up willingly, I killed. When I was in my twenties I was caught and put in prison.

In those days you didn't just walk down a hallway to your death, they made a parade and you were the attraction. People came with rocks and trash and thorns and you had to hike it five miles.

I remember the nails. Big black spikes. I watched the guard as he lined one up on my wrist and I realized that he was probably killing me with my father's nails.

I kept seeing Judah's face in front of me. It was like he was in the crowd and behind the guard and in the clouds. He was watching me die. I didn't know either of the two men who were being crucified along with me. I had heard the rabbi preach. He was a storyteller. They said he was trouble and that he was trying to overthrow the government. They said he was the Messiah.

Hanging there is a pain I can't describe to you. The detectives said that Dontay was dead before he was nailed to the cross on my balcony. I thank God for that.

I had seen crucifixions before. Some people go mad in those last minutes. I think that's what happened to that other man. He started raving.

I just wanted to die. I just wanted my life to end. Every face I had hurt was in front of me. It started to rain and it felt like every drop of water hitting my skin was burning me. I remember banging my head against the cross trying to knock myself unconscious.

Then the madman started raging at the rabbi. I would have given anything for a lungful of air at the point. I turned and looked at them. I pushed myself up on the nail in my foot and felt a bone break. I told him to shut up.

Then the rabbi looked at me. His face had been beaten so that one eye was closed, but the other one that looked into my face...looked into my soul. I believed he was who he said he was. All those years of denying that the Messiah was coming, denying everything I had been taught, and now it was all true, and he was dying next to me.

I said, "Jesus. Would you remember me?"

I swear he smiled. Like somewhere down deep beneath his agony he thought of something funny. He smiled a bloody smile at me and that was the last thing I remembered. That smile. And the smell of smoke.

I think of where I could be when I smell smoke. I pick on Gabriel and give him a hard time but I am so grateful that I am what I am. I have touched the face of God and it was crying.

I stood on the roof of the church. Just to my right and one floor below was the balcony. I could still see the blood on the floor. Dontay's blood. I could still see the crime scene tape. I breathed in the smoke from fires around the city and it filled me. The man who nailed Dontay to pieces of wood was waiting for me down the street. I thought of Dontay when I stepped off the roof.

CHAPTER FORTY-ONE

Cantrell was in a rage. He hadn't done his own dirty work in years. This was the old Cantrell, the one before his promotion. This was the Cantrell who did things himself. "Do it yourself," he thought in his anger. "Leave no witnesses, no trail. Nobody who can point your ass out in court." He had the cab driver drop him off three blocks from the church. *A cab*. He hadn't ridden in a cab in years. He missed his car. He stepped out of the cab into the cold air, his rage keeping him warm, his rage propelling him along the street toward the church. He looked up at the dark building. There was light behind the stained glass windows. There was a single light over the door. Cantrell saw the figure in the third floor office. Fucking priest. Fucking troublemaker. Fucking dead. These were Cantrell's thoughts as he crossed the street to the church entrance.

He didn't bother to check the door as he picked up a garbage can and raised it over his head. The glass in the doorway shattered. There was no alarm. Thump had told him that. Thump the traitor. Thump the asshole. Thump the soon-to-be-dead Thump. After he put a bullet in the priest, he planned to put several in Thump. Probably take a full clip just to put him down.

Cantrell kicked away the glass and stepped inside. The cameras were phonies. Thump had learned that as well.

The elevator took him to the third floor. He pulled the gun out of his pants as he stepped off the elevator. The hallway was dark except for the one office. Cantrell stepped into the office ready to shoot.

The girl at the window turned and screamed.

CHAPTER FORTY-TWO

The smoke on the wind filled Micah's nostrils as the current passed under the thick matted feathers of his wings. He soared around the roof of the building twice looking for movement or shadow to go along with the feeling of evil's presence. Something was there.

Landing hard on the roof, the gravel and concrete beneath the thick leathery soles of his feet, he folded the massive wings behind his back. Micah closed his eyes and reached out with his mind. He smelled the city. He heard the wind. He felt the vibration beneath his feet as an electrical generator kicked on. Micah took it as an invitation.

Micah walked down the ramp from the roof into the dark parking garage, the only illumination being the battery-operated security lights over the door and the moon outside. Walking down into the darkness, he was briefly reminded of the mouth of hell, which he had seen but had not entered.

He reached out with himself, the ebony feathers

in his wings bristling. The sound of the generator was louder now. Thump was here. Thump was waiting.

Wires and cables hung from the ceiling on this floor. The tips of his wings brushed along the plastic sheeting which had been tacked in place to keep the exposed electrical system dry. Micah smelled oil, and garbage, and sweat.

He rounded the corner and heard a loud sharp "huffff" sound as the first nail from the air-gun entered his left shoulder. Micah roared and clutched at the small metal spike in his flesh. He yanked it out. The second whizzed past his left ear. The third shot through the thin membrane of skin in his wing. He turned toward Thump who was taking aim again. Micah put his hand up reflexively and the spike entered his right forearm instead of his left eye.

He opened himself up to his full size and ran toward the man with the nail gun held to his shoulder like a rocket launcher. Micah picked up a 2x4 from a stack of scrap pieces. He would reason later that this is where the wood from Dontay's cross had come from. In this moment there was no reason. In this moment there was rage. Micah raised the wood over his head as Thump removed the pistol from his belt and fired.

The bullet entered the beast's belly just below the rib cage. It chipped bone and came out the other side. Screaming, Micah swung the 2x4, connecting with Thump's side. Thump shouted and dropped the nail gun, which fired two shots as it hit the *cement floor. The first entered the wall. The second glanced off and lay on the floor where it would remain for the next few months before puncturing the tire of a 60-year-old CEO who had just prayed to God for a sign about whether or not to retire.*

Thump hit the ground and rolled out of the way as the wooden plank came down where his head had been. He raised the gun again and the beast kicked it out of his hand. The thing grabbed him by the throat and lifted him off the floor.

"Whatthefuckareyou?" Thump said, his eyes wide and angry.

Micah brought him in close to answer, and Thump kicked him hard where the bullet had pierced his side.

He howled and dropped the former gang-banger turned businessman. He was on his feet and ran. Micah followed. Thump pulled down wires and sheeting and knocked over carts of equipment .

Micah pushed away a thick black sheet of plastic as Thump threw the hammer. It glanced off the side of Micah's head and he growled.

"Whatthefuckareyou?" Thump shouted, this time, it was not out of fear but from anger and hatred.

Micah leapt at the man, the nails of his hand tearing the cotton of Thump's black jacket. Micah could feel where he had scratched the skin. Thump yelled but he kept running. He ran toward the concrete pilings that supported the floors above him. He squeezed himself through, thinking perhaps that the thing was too big to follow and would have to take the long way around. He didn't stop to see if his risk had paid off. He had wounded it. Perhaps it would fall back and regroup. Thump had a sudden memory of Dontay hanging on the cross, and he doubted that the thing was going to stop.

Hearing only his own footsteps echo in the dark, he rounded the last corner and saw the open street ahead of him. He could see the lights from across the street reflecting on the wet pavement. He could hear the engine of the late night bus. He was twenty feet away from the exit when the thing dropped out of the sky and landed heavily on the sidewalk in his path. Thump realized he had been running from an enemy with wings and he had just led it out into the open. Business Practices of the Samurai Warrior *had never covered what to do if your opponent has wings.*

"WHAT THE FUCK ARE YOU?" he screamed, finally recovering his diction in his rage.

The gargoyle made no sound at all. It opened its wings. It smiled, lips pulling back from too many sharp teeth. Thump opened his bladder.

Thump stared as the creature in front of him reached into the pocket of its long black coat and pulled out handful of clean silver nails, each the size and length of a pencil.

Thump laughed. "Fucker don't have a nail gun. Don't have a compressor."

Micah tilted his head. His voice made Thump's stomach drop. "Fucker don't need one."

CHAPTER FORTY-THREE

Padi, who had dialed 911 on not one, but all of the cell phones that Father Michael had given her before dropping them from the window into the trash bin below, had screamed like a little girl when Cantrell entered the room. She would later tell herself that she had done this to fake him out. In fact, that was her plan when she saw him was coming into the building, but when the scream finally came out of her throat it was much more real-sounding to her than she wanted it to be.

The dumpster was open three floors below and she had dialed the emergency number and then dropped them one by one into the bin. The first one shattered on the side of the metal box. She remembered the game from birthday parties where she had to drop old fashioned wooden clothespins into a bottle. Her father had told her the secret was to aim with your nose. Padi dialed 911 on the second phone, then dropped it, scoring a perfect hit as the phone landed on the plastic garbage bags. "Score!" she said.

When the man with the gun came into the office, she assumed this was the one called Cantrell, simply because of how angry he was. She had been reading a lot about him in the files from the pony flash drive. She also assumed he had something to do with Dontay's death. She decided then and there that, if she could, she was going to hurt him very, very badly.

After her way-too-girlie scream he came into the room and pointed the gun at her head.

She hesitated and he tilted his gun and his head at the same time. "I will kill you," he said, "then I will shoot the priest. Then I will set fire to this building. Do you believe I will do these things?" Padi nodded. "Good," Cantrell said. "I hate to repeat myself."

He forced her into the elevator and to the top floor of the building. She had been here before. Every kid who had grown up in the church knew about this floor. It was a rite of passage. Can you go up to the haunted floor and come down the fire escape on the other side? Every possible variation of the murdering ghost of the seminarian who had butchered the other student had been told at countless Halloween parties. Every kid knew the real reason they'd had to close off the dormitories in the 50s. The real reason, of course, was money and lack of students, but that didn't stop rumors and legends from spreading. The fifth floor was the perfect setting for ghost stories and secret make-out sessions.

In the elevator the man with the gun had made

her stand in front of him. "We're going to the roof," he said. The doors opened and the dark hallway waited for them, the first six feet or so illuminated by the light of the elevator. He put the gun against the back of her head and with his free hand punched the hold button on the elevator panel. No bells rung. No sirens blared. "How'd this place ever get past code?" he wondered.

He pushed her head forward with the barrel of the gun and said, "Move." She started walking. The fourth room down from the corner of the building led to a fire escape that would lead them to the roof. She didn't think that he meant to make her jump. She knew he didn't mean to kill her at all or else he would have done so by now. He was using her to get something else.

She half prayed that the door would be locked when she tried, but it never was. Thick dust came up from the floor of the room that was being used to house the Christmas decorations.

"Lights?" Cantrell asked. Padi reached into the room and felt along the wall until she found the switch. Only one of the six fluorescent bulbs housed in the ceiling blinked on. It fluttered, creating a headache-inducing strobe effect. Finally the light solidified. In the corner someone had pulled the life-sized plastic light-up angel out of the box and set her on top of an army-green filing cabinet. A Magic Marker had been used to give her innocent face a black goatee and horns.

"Open the window and walk up the stairs until I tell you to stop." Padi did exactly as she was told.

The cold November air bit into her arms as she opened the window. The wind blew the dust around in the room. She stepped through and, without looking back at him, she started up the fire escape. "That's far enough," Cantrell said.

He crawled through the window himself and never once took his eyes off the girl. "You seem smart enough to know not to do something stupid."

Padi nodded, wondering if he saw the irony in his statement. Then she wondered if he knew what irony meant.

"We're going up to the roof," Cantrell said. "You first."

Padi grabbed hold of the cold metal railing and began to climb the rest of the way to the roof.

"Stay right there," Cantrell said. Padi froze in place.

Cantrell followed her over the edge of the building and onto the tarpaper-and-gravel rooftop. His suit was now filthy. After getting his feet under him, Cantrell grabbed Padi by the arm and walked her to the middle of the roof. Cantrell squeezed her arm tight so she wouldn't bolt away, and then looked up at the sky. "It's you and me, Fuck-face," he shouted. "I got your little girlfriend here. So, show your ugly face."

There was an uneasy bump behind them and a rustling of what sounded like someone flapping wet canvas in a strong wind. Cantrell turned with Padi's arm still in his hand.

The first time Dontay had told her about the creature, she hadn't believed him. He had told her what it had done to him, and how it looked, and how it smelled. When she saw it on the street, when it had spoken to her, she had been horrified. She didn't trust any of her memories as to what the thing actually looked like. Such a thing was not possible. Padi believed all things were possible now.

The gargoyle demon was real.

It was in front of them.

And it was very, very pissed.

The thing reared its head back and roared loudly. This time, when Padi screamed it came from somewhere down deep in the places people don't talk about.

Cantrell said, "Holy shit," but did not let go of her arm.

The thing sat squat on the edge of the bulding, its huge arms hanging down in front of it. A line of spit dripped down onto the black roof, and both Padi and Cantrell simultaneously thought it would smoke and burn there.

From the street, all three of them heard the sirens. Micah looked at Padi and she smirked, just a little.

Cantrell put the barrel of the gun to the back of Padi's head. Micah stood up and raised his wings. Cantrell saw the blood on the front of his shirt. "Heh, looks like you and Thump have already had a chat."

Micah tilted his head to one side. "I think his last

words were 'AAAAAAAAAAAAAAHHHHHHH-
HHHHHHHHH.'"
Cantrell smiled. "No loss. Gimme the drive."

* * *

On the street below, Detective Maggie Grafton
threw open the car door and stepped out.

She looked at the broken door of the church and
said, "Shit. Sergeant." A graying uniformed cop
turned to look at her. "This is the place. Three cells
all calling nine-one-one from this location."

Grafton looked up. The sergeant followed her
gaze and they saw the gargoyles on the roof of the
church. One of them moved. "Shit. Shit," she said
again, and ran for the front door.

* * *

Micah stood fifteen feet from Cantrell. He
walked cautiously along the edge of the roof where
the building faced the back alley.

"I swear I'll kill her," Cantrell said. "You're
gonna give me the drive and then you and your big
fucking wings are going to fly us all outta here."

Micah stared at Cantrell and then at Padi. He
reached into the breast pocket of his coat. Cantrell
pushed the gun harder into Padi's head. Padi yelped
in pain. The gargoyle slowly pulled the plastic toy
out of his pocket and held it between two fingers.
He walked forward two steps and set the little blue
pony on the roof, then backed carefully away.

Cantrell eased his grip on Padi's arm and brought his face close to her ear. "Pick it up. You try anything and I'll splatter blood all over your pretty hair."

Padi inched forward and bent low to pick up the flash drive.

"What's it say on it?" Cantrell said.

"My Little Fucking Pony," Padi said. Her voice quivered way more than she wanted it to.

Her bravery stunned Micah, but he smiled just a little. It was not a pleasant smile.

"That's mine." Cantrell said behind her. "You think I'm going to write 'crime files' on a regular flash drive? Hand it to me." Cantrell said. Padi held it behind her, never taking her eyes off the giant just four feet in front of her now. Cantrell took the flash drive from her hand and slid it into his own jacket pocket. Padi stared at the dark scary angel that towered in front of her. Slowly its lips curled back from its many, many teeth. Between its jaws it held a single peanut M&M. Yellow. Padi's eyes grew wide.

"Now, then..." Cantrell started.

Micah lunged forward and grabbed her. In one easy move he tossed her over the edge of the building. She screamed but only briefly.

Cantrell looked at him in disbelief. "What the..." was all he managed to get out before Micah batted the gun out of his hand and lifted him off the ground.

Micah carried Cantrell over to the side of the building and held him out over the edge. "You killed her? I don't fucking believe you did that," Cantrell said. The front of his shirt began to smoke, and Cantrell was suddenly very, very scared.

"Police! Hold it!" Micah looked and saw five armed cops. They were all pointing guns at him.

"Put him down." This voice was Maggie Grafton's. She had climbed over the edge of the fire escape and was aiming her pistol as well. "Put him down," she said.

Cantrell struggled against the massive grip. He said, "Help me, officer." He even managed to sound scared. "That thing just killed a little girl."

Micah turned toward Maggie, and she saw his face for the first time. "Holy Mother of God." Maggie said.

Micah turned back toward Cantrell. Cantrell continued to act terrified, but he locked eyes with Micah and his eyes were laughing. The beast brought Cantrell's face in close and said, "You wanna go for a ride?"

With that Micah spread his black wings and jumped off the top of the building. Two of the officers who had climbed onto the roof with the detective fired.

"Hold your fire!" Grafton said.

They stood there and watched. One cop said "But, Detective..."

"Whatever that was," the detective said, "it was holding a citizen of this city and you might hit him." They watched as it disappeared into the blackness of the sky. "Radio downstairs," Grafton said. "Find out if they saw which way it went."

They started back to the fire escape when they heard, "*Hey.*"

Grafton and the sergeant looked at each other.

They heard it again. "*Heyyyy.*"

Both ran to the edge of the building and looked over the edge. About fifteen feet down a teen-aged girl lay on her back on a small balcony that jutted out from the side of the building.

Grafton said, "Who the hell are you?"

Padi said, "Who the hell are *you?*"

CHAPTER FORTY-FOUR

The Penner Building was the tallest building in Philadelphia. It opened for business in 2000. Eighteen floors, and every office occupied at the grand opening. The 16th floor was home to the offices of real estate magnate Chris Moore, who was also a Councilman for the 7th district. He was still standing at his window, watching the smoke from the fires that turned out to be not nearly as bad as they looked.

On the roof of the building, Cantrell felt the cold brick against his back. He had passed out during the their flight, and now awoke to find himself upside down looking at the ground. Cantrell suddenly screamed, a little girlie scream that would have made Padi feel much better if she had been there to hear it.

For the first time, the monster smiled. "Say hello to the Councilman on your way by."

"Noooooooooo," Cantrell said.

"Micah," a voice said. Micah knew from the

glow who was behind him, even before he turned.

"Not now," Micah said.

"Micah," Gabriel said again. Still clutching the dealer's ankle, Micah turned. Gabriel was sitting...no, not really sitting...he was in a seated position...hovering just above an air duct.

Micah opened his mouth to say something, but then shut it.

"Micah. That's not how we do things," said the angel in white.

"It's how I do things," said the angel in black.

"Micah," the angel said again.

Micah sighed heavily and pulled Cantrell up and dropped him on his head on the roof. Cantrell struggled and got to his feet. He made no attempt to run. Standing there looking up into the face of the monster Cantrell shouted, "I thought you had balls. I though you had a pair. You think you scare me, Fuck-face. You think you scare me? You don't scare me! Think you can kill me? I'll see you in hell!"

Micah suddenly clapped two massive hands on either side of Cantrell's head. "You want to know what hell is?"

In one instant, Micah allowed Cantrell's soul to drop out of his body and plummet into a realm where no human had been and come back. As if it were on a bungee cord, Cantrell's soul shot back up and into his body. His eyes refocused for just a moment on Micah's face and then turned absolutely white.

Later when they discovered him on the roof and

rushed him to the hospital, the emergency room physician would think that the man's eyeballs had somehow come detached and had rolled back to the point of blindness. An ocular surgeon was called in and after examination stated that the man had no iris and no pupil and that this defect was probably something the man had since birth but he could not remember the name of the condition. In fact he spent the next week trying to find such a condition but never did.

The man had no wallet, no keys, no identification of any kind—and, since he never actually woke up again, he provided no information on his own. He was remanded to a welfare hospital, where he slept in perpetual nightmare for the rest of his days.

Leaving Cantrell's twitching body on the roof, Micah crawled on the outside of the building lowering himself down several floors until he poked his head out and saw Councilman Moore. Moore jumped backward and fell over a guest chair. Micah waited for him to stand and inch closer to the window. With one hand clinging tightly to the ledge, Micah reached into his coat with the other hand and pulled out a colorful plastic pony which he waved back and forth in front of the councilman on the other side of the glass.

Moore watched the creature's lips pull back from its teeth in a horrid smile that made his skin crawl. The creature put the toy back in its coat. It let go of the side of the building and dropped like a stone out of sight. Moore ran to the window and saw the beast, with wings fully spread, fly off in the direction of the bridge.

CHAPTER FORTY-FIVE

The cop who stopped me on the street was Officer Timmy. I shit you not. Officer Timmy. On the upside, he was a huge guy so I doubt he got razzed about it too much. Kind of like Father Dark. People look at you and smirk a little. You smile and nod and let them know it's okay and they let it go. Officer Timmy was a big man. Bigger than my friend Thump...or maybe bigger than my friend Thump *was*. I must pay a clerical call on Roberta later today.

The street outside of the church was bathed in red and blue flashing lights. A dozen cop cars lined the street. I wish I had told Dwight to stay late. He could have cleaned up. Cops and coffee.

Officer Timmy held up a big meaty hand as I rounded the corner and tried to look surprised. "Sir, this street is blocked off, I'm afraid you'll have to..."

I interrupted him. "I'm Father Michael, from Saint Marjorie's.... Oh, God, has there been another incident?"

"You'll want to come with me, Father."

I followed him. Mental note: next time, you stash clothes someplace for a quick change. Remember socks. November in Philadelphia is a bit brisk.

Officer Timmy led me toward an ambulance. I saw Padi sitting in the back sipping coffee. She had a blanket around her shoulders and was giving a serious flirty face to the ambulance driver. He had dreads. Must remember to tell Gabriel to let me have dreads sometimes. If he ever lets me come back again.

Detective Maggie Grafton stood by the ambulance. One hand was on her hip pushing her long coat back. I could see her revolver and her badge clipped to her belt. Like I said, there's something about powerful women that just does it for me. She looked like she was wearing yesterday's clothes she'd kicked into the hamper and then pulled out when the call came in. I wonder what that call was like. I wonder if she had come up with a rational explanation for what she saw on the roof. Then the thought of her putting on yesterdays clothes came back again and made me wonder what she wore to bed. I waited for the mental pinch from Gabriel to tell me I was being inappropriate. Feeling none, I continued to picture the detective in her night things as Officer Timmy led me closer. Grafton's red hair was made even redder by the lights on top of the patrol car.

Timmy asked, "Detective Grafton?"

Grafton looked up. So did Padi. I wasn't sure

what sort of reaction I was going to get from her, but her bravery kicked in and she smiled at me. I ran forward and hugged her tight. "Oh, God. I was so afraid. I saw the lights and I thought..."

I pulled her away so I could look at her in a kind priestly way, and hugged her again. "I thought something else had happened. What the hell are you doing here?"

She said, "Father Dark, do you have any coffee up in your apartment? This is nasty."

"Dwight's opens in the morning. I'll buy you one of those hot-candy-bars-in-a-cup you seem to enjoy."

Padi said, "It is morning."

Detective Grafton was looking at me as if she were impatiently waiting for us to finish. She looked at me over the rim of her glasses. She hadn't been wearing those when we talked earlier. Did I mention I have a thing about librarians too? She said, "Where were you tonight, Father?"

I pulled a grease-stained paper bag from the pocket of my coat. "Cheese steak," I said. "Why, what did I miss this time?"

CHAPTER FORTY-SIX

It was four-thirty in the morning (three hours after what happened on the church roof) when Miss Roberta was awakened by a sound at her window. It was a tapping sound. Not an intentional tap-tap-tap but more like something blowing against it in the wind. Her tiny apartment was on the 14th floor, and she didn't get a lot of visitors this way, so she didn't think twice about opening the curtains.

She did not scream. She would later give herself that much credit. Even though she could have screamed, and said later that she did not, and no one would have been the wiser. She did not scream.

Hanging outside her window was a man wrapped in duct tape. He was covered nearly head-to-toe, and suspended by his feet from a thick nylon yellow rope. The man was awake and looked at her, his eyes expressionless. As his body spun in place, Roberta could see two nails sticking through each of the man's wrists. The back of his shirt was drenched in his own blood. She opened the window and attempted to spin his bulky frame around and bring him into her apartment. Tied to the man's belt was a large utility knife. Stapled to his shirt front was a sheet of paper. In black Magic Marker were the words "He Killed Your Grandson."

Roberta yanked the paper, only then realizing the note had been stapled to the man's skin. He grunted through the tape covering his mouth.

Roberta held the note to his face. He tilted his head and she turned the note upside-down so he could read it. His eyes grew wider.

Roberta, who had seen her own husband beaten to death by dealers in 1977—

Roberta who had watched her daughter slide into a coma after an overdose—

Roberta who had raised and wept over her grandson—

Roberta who had rejoiced and thanked God for the new priest who seemed to be opening new doors for her last remaining relative—

—grabbed the knife and used it to cut the short piece of cord that held it to the big man's belt. She bent low and showed the knife to the man, whose tears were now falling up and rolling across his forehead.

She waited to speak until she had his full attention. She asked, "Do you believe in God?"

CHAPTER FORTY-SEVEN

A STAR OVER THE I (EYE)
A blog about nothing, written for no one in particular, by someone who pretty much stopped giving a rat's ass about things a long time ago.

ENTRY: 670
There is a giant scary gargoyle thing flying around Philadelphia at night. Yes, Dr. Conners, I can say that because it's true. I saw it. It likes M&Ms. Also true.

Yes, I still go to church. More so.

Yes, I believe in God. More so.

Yes, I am on a first-name basis with a Philadelphia Detective. Her name is Maggie, and she had Thanksgiving dinner at my house...with my priest...both of my priests, actually. Dontay's grandma came too. Mom didn't burn the turkey and the sweet potato casserole was fairly decent.

Yes, if you make fun of me for going to church I will still flip you the bird.

Yes, I miss my friend Dontay.

Yes, I feel I have rehabilitated myself and have seen the error of my previous hacking ways and have kept my nose clean. I think the time I have spent working with Fr. Dark has contributed to my rehabilitation, and would like to be let off of probation now.

Yes, I will keep the blog going even if the only ones who read it are my court-ordered counselor, my priest, and my mother. Yes, Mom, I know you are stalking me. Maybe you can print this one out and hang in on the fridge next to the one and only 100% I ever got on a spelling test...*in third grade.*

I'm going to sign off now. It's time for *My Little Pony.*

I'm going to church this afternoon. Fr. Dark says he's had some ideas for opening a kind of shelter and I'm up for that.